S0-AIJ-164

# The Promise of Blood

As Carter and Margo Huerta started down the steps toward the rear garage, Carter began to realize why he'd been suspicious. There were five of them, arranged in two groups so that on first look it would appear to be a group of garage mechanics talking or, even more innocently, a bunch of teenagers. They were all relatively short and wiry.

Carter assessed them quickly.

They were good with feet, hands, or weapons.

They were lethal and ready...

# NICK CARTER IS IT!

"Nick Carter out-Bonds James Bond."
—*Buffalo Evening News*

"Nick Carter is America's #1 espionage agent."
—*Variety*

"Nick Carter is razor-sharp suspense."
—*King Features*

"Nick Carter has attracted an army of addicted readers ... the books are fast, have plenty of action and just the right degree of sex ... Nick Carter is the American James Bond, suave, sophisticated, a killer with both the ladies and the enemy."
—*The New York Times*

# FROM THE NICK CARTER
# KILLMASTER SERIES

LAW OF THE LION

# KILL MASTER

# NICK CARTER

JOVE BOOKS, NEW YORK

"Nick Carter" is a registered trademark of The Condé Nast
Publications, Inc., registered in the United States Patent Office.

KILLMASTER #252: LAW OF THE LION

A Jove Book/published by arrangement with
The Condé Nast Publications, Inc.

PRINTING HISTORY
Jove edition/August 1989

All rights reserved.
Copyright © 1989 by The Condé Nast Publications, Inc.
This book may not be reproduced in whole or in part,
by mimeograph or any other means, without permission.
For information address: The Berkley Publishing Group,
200 Madison Avenue, New York, New York 10016.

ISBN: 0-515-10106-0

Jove Books are published by The Berkley Publishing Group,
200 Madison Avenue, New York, New York 10016.
The name "JOVE" and the "J" logo
are trademarks belonging to Jove Publications, Inc.

PRINTED IN THE UNITED STATES OF AMERICA

10 9 8 7 6 5 4 3 2 1

*Dedicated to the men and women of the
Secret Services of the
United States of America*

LAW OF THE LION

# KILL MASTER

# ONE

*San Salvador, El Salvador*

John Merton set up his equipment in the small, neatly manicured park just beyond the Sheraton El Salvador, at a comfortable distance from the boxlike encroachments of the shantytown and even less formal street camps and cooking fires that had sprung up like mushrooms along the main roads to the central city.

He fiddled with the dial of his ghetto blaster, switching quickly from some piercing rhetoric about the forthcoming elections to a musical lament sung by a man who was complaining that his señorita had lost that lovin' feeling. Moving the dial a bit more toward 88.1 MHz, he got what he really wanted: talk radio that was no part of the ordinary broadcast band. Instead, Merton tuned in on an animated conversation among three men sitting at a sprawling sidewalk café about half a block away.

Dressed as a tourist, Merton had comfortable walking shoes, a new white guayabera shirt, and an auto-everything camera. The shoeshine kids and the young girls selling packets of gum were swarming over him and that was just fine. Tourist they wanted, tourist they'd get. It gave him just the kind of cover he wanted. The tape cassette in the ghetto blaster was recording the conversation of his quarries, two *contra* captains wanting to "invest" some American humanitarian relief funds. They were joined by a skinny little guy who was showing them floor plans and a prospectus for a condo in Fort Lauderdale. Of course, if the two illustrious *contradores* were serious about wanting a completely different kind of climate than the tropics, why here was a splendid deal in Mammoth, California, that included an unlimited lift ticket during ski season.

Merton smiled. This was great equipment and an even greater opportunity to nail two leeches who abused their power to further their own personal fortunes.

It was all going down beautifully and he was getting it. One of the more satisfying pieces of work in some time.

And then a tortured stage whisper sounded behind him. "I've got to talk to you, Merton."

The mention of his name jabbed like a beesting. Merton turned to see a man in his late forties lurching toward him, the latest in the procession of people wanting to sell the gringo something. Only this shambling, stumbling drunk was no stranger, not really a drunk. His eyes blazed with conviction. "Please."

"You idiot," Merton hissed. "I'm working."

"This is front-rank stuff," the man said. "Worth risking whatever you've got going down."

"Your credibility is all used up, Prentiss."

"I'm not selling this time," Prentiss said, "I'm giving. No strings. This is to buy back my self-respect."

"Your so-called self-respect could get us killed. Now bug off."

"This will show you how serious I am." Prentiss calculated the trajectory, then tossed a small chamois pouch toward Merton. When the pouch landed, two uncut diamonds the size of robin's eggs tumbled forth.

Before Merton could adjust to this development, a well-built man in jeans and a black T-shirt emerged from behind some shrubbery, snapping a modification in place on an AR-15 Colt with well-practiced ease, converting it to the power of an M-16. He, too, had sound equipment—what appeared to be a Walkman with an earplug. "Merton's right, Prentiss. Your self-respect has gotten you killed." He put a short burst in Merton's chest. An equally short burst caught Prentiss in the throat.

While the assailant moved in to scoop up the diamonds, Prentiss managed to trace two letters—*LT*—in the ground before him, roll over on top of them, and die.

•   •   •

*Covington, Kentucky*

Sam Zachary still wasn't sure how much of Sheriff Shelton's good-old-boy routine was real or how far he ought to push the sheriff in order to find out. Big fellow, dressed right out of a Banana Republic catalogue. Flop-brimmed Aussie hat. Right foot wrapped in several yards of beige Ace bandage. Could be an occupation-related wound. But judging by the way the sheriff liked to eat, it could also be old-fashioned gout.

No question about Milner, the general manager of the River View Inn. Aviator-type sunglasses, white tassel loafers, knit shirt complete with tiny alligator, a tennis sweater draped over his shoulders. In all probability he used Grecian Formula to keep the boyish, earnest young jock effect suggested by his razor-cut light brown hair. Zachary almost gagged when he caught the pinky ring with a baby blue stone.

"One more time, just to make sure I get it," Sam Zachary said. "You have no idea where Arriosto's body is now, and no one"—he looked meaningfully at Sheriff Shelton—"no one kept tabs on the little lady?" A tall man with a lean, runner's body, Zachary watched Milner giving him the once-over, checking out Zachary's gabardine twills and the lightweight blazer tailored on Savile Row.

"Miss Crystal," Milner said, wanting to be helpful

"No one kept tabs on Miss Crystal," Sheriff Shelton said, sounding, Zachary thought, as though he were explaining something to a small child. "No one kept tabs because we all felt she showed great responsibility, calling us in the first place."

Zachary started counting to ten.

"That little lady gave mouth-to-mouth resuscitation and even tried the Heimlich maneuver," Sheriff Shelton continued. "She stuck around until we arrived and pronounced the, uh, the guest dead of apparently natural causes." There was a great, resonant sadness in his voice.

"Is that what you folks call it around here, 'apparently natural causes'? Any tourist who dies in Covington, it's natural?" Zachary stared at Sheriff Shelton. "Hey, I can understand an attitude like that, but the truth in this case is another matter. We'll never know about the cause of death if the body is missing and we can't do an autopsy."

Sam Zachary looked about the deluxe garden suite where Guillermo Arriosto had died. Lots of empty bottles lying around. Good booze. Glenlivet. Stolichnaya. Several brands of beer. Any number of foreign brands as well as Hudephol, a quite acceptable local beer from nearby Cincinnati. Good snacks.

Zachary got up and poked idly about the king-sized bed. He looked up at the round mirror on the ceiling. A large color TV set had a huge placard announcing that you weren't limited to such ordinary fare as dish antenna and cable TV stuff. You could have adult entertainment simply by turning the TV dial to 3 and following the simple instructions.

There was lots of lingerie draped all over the place. Sam Zachary lifted a black stocking. Real silk from the feel of it. Arriosto had liked his pleasures. "Looks like the little lady left in a hurry."

"Actually," Milner said, "she was wearing—she was completely dressed when she left. I think Mr. Arriosto brought this and other accouterments with him."

"And you say he paid for everything in cash? No credit cards?"

"All cash," Milner said, nodding. "When he checked in, he told us what his requirements were and I thought a cash transaction would be the best for all of us."

"When he mentioned his, uh, requirements," Zachary said, "did they include this young lady? Miss Crystal?"

Sheriff Shelton stood, gingerly resting his weight on a cane and trying to protect his right foot. The big fellow seemed agile in spite of his problem. "We've been pretty straight with you, Zachary. For my part, I can't help wondering why the Justice Department should be so interested in an apparently natural occurrence. We make no bones about the entertainment available here in Covington. A man runs a successful car dealership in Phoenix and wants to come here and cut loose, we like to see he gets his money's worth. We like to cooperate, but it seems to me the Justice people have no jurisdiction in this—this apparently sad case where a man simply bit off more than he could chew."

Zachary snapped his fingers. "Rats. Sheriff, you've got me, pure and simple. You let me climb out on a limb, and you sawed it off. We have no jurisdiction. But we do have plenty of clout with law enforcement groups who'd be interested in the fact that Miss Crystal—if that's her real name—is only fifteen."

"Sixteen," Milner said. "And the record should also show that Mr. Arriosto got everything he paid for and that we have all his personal belongings."

Yeah, no question about it. Emboldened by the revelation that Zachary had no jurisdiction, Milner was trying to come on feisty, no preppy wimp he, by God. If it ever came down to it, Milner would fall over when he discovered that Zachary didn't even work for the Justice Department. People in the continental U.S. always seemed outraged when they had direct dealings with someone from the Agency.

Well, the hell with it, Zachary thought. He'd had enough of this. He snapped his notebook shut, content with his reading of the facts in the case.

Guillermo Arriosto was supposed to be a car salesman from Phoenix. Supposed to be is right. It didn't matter if he actually sold a car or not.

In reality, he was a military man from Argentina who'd been given a laundered identity by the CIA, whisked out of his country (just in time to avoid some serious legal stuff), and plugged into the good life in the American Southwest.

Sure, Arriosto had a good dealership, and he worked it with some energy. He put that little drawing of an Argentine cowboy on his business card and called himself the Grinning Gaucho.

But the Agency had paid plenty to set it up and structure the business so that Arriosto would net at least fifty, sixty thou a year—Arriosto had insisted on that no matter how the dealership did. And there had been a few unsecured loans for a series of TV ads he'd wanted to run, to get people to start talking about his dealership, Arriosto had said.

Okay, this guy came here to Covington, held a number of private meetings in this suite with a number of unidentified associates, and then, when the meetings were finished and his visitors were gone, he'd sent out for a long-legged sixteen-year-old hooker. After a day with Miss Crystal, Arriosto's heart had given out, or so it seemed if one bought the Covington version.

Sheriff Shelton and Milner had really gone to some lengths

to cover their tails on this one, and had sent the body to a small private hospital. Zachary could put the squeeze on them by asking how it was that they had so suddenly become so concerned about a corpse.

What they'd done, Shelton and Milner, was to summon a high-powered forensic man from the medical school in Cincinnati, probably some guy who had his own reasons for coming over the bridge to Covington from time to time, to do the postmortem.

But before the doctor arrived, Arriosto's mortal remains had been snatched by person or persons unknown.

No witnesses. No clues. Just gone with no forwarding address.

Sure, Zachary could make a thing out of questioning the cleaning women, even try to find out which of the bellboys had brought over some of the snacks and drinks. Since Covington was so free-swinging, there might even be a friendly neighborhood pimp who saw something.

But they were all probably wired into the routine in Covington, and had long since learned that it was worth their job not to notice or remember anything except what the customers wanted.

There was no reason to think Shelton and Milner weren't telling the truth. They could have tried a complete cover-up or at least planted a few things to take some of the heat off of them.

Zachary decided to punch it to the manager. "What you're saying, bottom line, Mr. Milner, is that people with ethnic names can come to Covington, register in a place like this, provided they have enough money, and not have to worry about being rolled."

Milner moved his glasses up on the bridge of his nose by scowling. "You don't have to be so crude," he said.

Zachary still wasn't going to let him off the hook. "As a matter of fact, in my line of work," he said, "I sometimes have to be very crude."

You had to hand it to Milner, Zachary mused. He stood right there and took it, just as though you got nowhere in life if you were too thin-skinned.

"I wonder—" he began.

Zachary lifted a bushy brow, silently telling the guy to go ahead.

"I wonder if you'd tell me where you bought your blazer."

Zachary gave Milner the big Rotary Club pat on the back. "I get all my duds at K-Mart, sport. Thanks for asking."

# TWO

Even in the off-season months, Paris is an exciting city, with a special luminous look and pulse about it. Nick Carter had his quarry well enough in sight to allow a small portion of his mind to revel in being back in one of the most exciting cities in the world. He also knew from direct experience that Paris could be one of the deadliest cities in the world when he was working.

Perhaps after he'd finished with this man, Nico Sichi, he could manage a few days here for R & R. Then he could keep his mind on the Paris of the songwriters instead of the Paris of the undertaker.

But first the work. This hadn't been an easy assignment.

Not only was Carter following Sichi, but two other professionals were working him, and both were good.

Carter made one of the pros as possible PLO. A man with a hatchet-sharp face, thick brows, and dark, ebony hair that was beginning to recede at the crown, giving the look of an unwanted monk's tonsure. In his forties, he was slightly over medium height, wiry thin with the exception of a gut that had begun to work its way over his waistline.

The professional had a number of outstanding physical features, perhaps too many for the needed anonymity to be a good intelligence agent. His chin was dimpled, his eyes bright blue-white disks, reminding Carter of a dog with cast eyes.

The other professional was definitely Mossad, Lev Abrams, a short, pouter pigeon of a man with curly reddish hair. Neither of the professionals was aware of the other, and Carter was sure they hadn't noticed him. At the moment, all eyes were on Sichi and his activities.

8

Mustached and dapper in a tan linen suit with paisley tie, Nico Sichi moved purposely to the newly restored Café de la Paix, with sidewalk service and a splendid view of the Place de l'Opéra.

At least he had good taste, Carter thought, picking a café Carter himself would have taken for an unhurried view of the city. Place de l'Opéra was more than a large intersection, it was the business, shopping, and theater heart of Paris, complex and ever fascinating as busy men and attractive women from the three different worlds bustled and interacted.

Carter saw a number of banks, noting that the number of Japanese ventures had increased since his last visit. There were tables filled with elegant-looking women who, to judge by the parcels set close at their feet, had been shopping at Aux Trois Quartiers or some of the other big department stores behind the opera house on Boulevard Haussmann.

Sichi sat at a back table near a large planter, gave his order to a waiter, shot the cuffs of his striped shirt, and crossed his legs with particular attention to the crease of his trousers. He was doing his best to look like one of the brokers who'd come from some of the nearby banks or the huge Paris stock exchange.

Carter was not fooled by the little terrorist's enjoyment of elegant clothing or his seemingly casual manner. A member of the infamous Red Brigade, Sichi had used a bomb-fitted attaché case similar to the one now set before him on the table to blow apart a meeting of Common Market diplomats in Marseille just two days earlier. That had made major newspaper and TV network coverage.

Watching Sichi sip his café espresso and smoke a pungent Balkan Sobrane cigarette, Carter yearned for one of his own specially blended cigarettes, but instead watched patiently, listening to the sounds of high-pitched horns and the explosive Gallic tempers of drivers who attempted to negotiate the various intersections that emptied into the Place de l'Opéra.

Carter's alarm watch shrilled his appointed hour to call his superior, David Hawk, for further instructions.

Keeping his quarry in view, Carter made for a phone booth with push-button dialing, where he encoded a number that connected him half a world away to Washington, D.C.

A brisk, businesslike voice answered on the first ring.

"Good timing, N3. Let me have your report." Hawk had been expecting him.

Carter could envision his superior, David Hawk, the director of AXE, thumbing an ancient lighter with a huge striking wheel, and applying the flame to one of those mummified-- appearing cigars that looked awful and smelled worse.

AXE, a small, highly specialized intelligence-gathering and special action agency, was located on Dupont Circle in Washington, D.C. A cover organization, Amalgamated Press and Wire Services, made an effective front. AXE was entirely separate from the NSC, the CIA, and even the Justice Department. Thanks to David Hawk's background of service, his uncompromising integrity, and his absolute disinterest in playing political games, AXE was able to go where the bureaucracies feared to tread. It was also able to accomplish what the bureaucracies only dreamed about.

Hawk was AXE's founder, rarely left Washington these days, and even more rarely left his glass-walled penthouse office atop the Amalgamated building. Carter was his top man in the field, designated N3 and licensed to kill in the service of his government.

"The subject is about three hundred yards from me," Carter reported. "He's drinking coffee and reading a copy of *Le Figaro*."

Hawk grunted. "I'd have thought him for a *Le Monde* man, myself. What else?"

In the background, Carter could hear the steady drone of professional voices. In his office, Hawk frequently watched an elaborate monitoring screen bringing him TV news feeds from the Amalgamated Press dish antennas not far from his penthouse. Hawk was always close to major news sources as vital stories broke in the world. But he was even closer to sources of information many a top reporter would kill for.

"The subject has two tails in addition to me," Carter said. "One is possibly the PLO operative, Abdul Samadhi—I'm not certain yet—and the other is definitely Mossad, an operative named Lev Abrams. The PLO guy definitely doesn't know about Abrams, and Abrams doesn't know about the PLO man."

"What's your judgment, Nick? Are either of them killers?"

"Both," Carter said. "If I anticipate your next question, I'd say to put your money on Abrams as the tougher of the two. The Palestinian seems desperate. In a contest, that would blow his edge."

"I'm tempted to give you a few more days to see how this develops," Hawk said, and Carter could almost feel his superior relent on a decision he'd already made. "But something vital is breaking, and I need you here to deal with it. If our suspicions are correct, this could become one of the most unholy alliances in recent times. I've booked you on the SST from Orly to Toronto at six-thirty your time. A private jet will take you from Toronto to Phoenix. If you can neutralize your quarry without making a scene, and do a thorough body search, you are authorized to do so. We prefer him dead, but it is not acceptable for you to miss the SST flight. Clear?"

"Perfectly," Carter said, noting that the Arab who was also on Sichi's tail crossed the busy multiple intersection and positioned himself not more than a hundred yards from Sichi.

Lev Abrams, the other professional tracking Sichi, now stood in a small coffee bar sipping an espresso. Carter still believed Abrams was unaware of the PLO man.

"I'll have some details in the private jet for you to read on the way to Phoenix," Hawk continued. "Meanwhile, here's some information to begin thinking about."

Carter clicked his mind into the right gear, using a technique given him by Ira Wein, a psychologist friend. The technique was a clever mixture of hypnosis and visualization, allowing Carter to see his mind as the modem attachment of a computer. "Ready and waiting," Carter said.

Hawk's voice, gruff and hardbitten, set forth the facts. Carter, with a near photographic memory tuned to openness and receptivity, took it all in. "We start with Guy Prentiss, a twenty-year man with the CIA. Good operative, but no stomach for the bureaucracy and paperwork. He set up as a freelance double, passing information both ways and having the satisfaction of injecting subtle sabotages into both sides. He made a good deal on the side and actually donated most of it to worthwhile causes. Mother Teresa. Greenpeace. Amnesty. As you've probably learned by now, things in our profession don't work that way. You can't buy out of betrayals with conscience money."

"Prentiss got caught up in ideologies?" Carter asked.

"Worse. He was pulled into a massive cocaine sting where he unwittingly betrayed friends on both sides." Hawk continued to relate how Prentiss, determined to redeem his conscience, had begun tracking something he considered to be of major consequence. He'd died trying to give it over to someone he trusted completely.

While he was being killed, Guy Prentiss had drawn a circle with the letters *LT* in it.

Hawk fired up his cold cigar and brought in a new piece of the puzzle. "We have some reports that promise to be most embarrassing to our friends in the Agency. Guillermo Arriosto, an auto dealer in Phoenix, Arizona, who called himself the Grinning Gaucho, died in Covington, Kentucky, of an apparent heart attack. Our information indicates that Arriosto was working on something rather large, global, and explosive."

Listening intently, Carter picked up more of the vital details: Arriosto had been relocated to Phoenix five years earlier with a laundered identity. His real name was Hector Cardenas. He'd been a colonel in the Argentine army. All official records showed Cardenas was dead, killed by leftist guerrillas before he could be brought to trial by the current Argentine administration.

"My theory," Hawk said, "is that the CIA was behind the theft of the body. I've been nudging them about it the past few hours."

"How did they respond to your probing, sir?"

"They were sensitive. I'll say this for them, they admitted it looked bad for them, but they denied any complicity."

"All the same, sir, it looks as though they couldn't stand the possibility that the results of the autopsy would be made public, showing their boy hadn't really been dead when he was supposed to be," Carter suggested.

"Exactly." Hawk paused to apply more flame to his cigar. "I also believe that Arriosto-Cardenas, now convincingly dead, was about to pull a fast one on his former benefactors, and they may have begun to get wind of it."

"And you think it has something to do with those initials?"

"Part of your assignment, Nick, is to make that connection for us or rule it out."

"And the rest of my assignment?"

Hawk filled Carter in on Miss Crystal. "No doubt about it, the Grinning Gaucho preferred them young. We even have information that his tastes brought him considerable trouble in Ciudad Juarez. The point is, Miss Crystal disappeared—gone from Covington without a trace. But get this—an older, champagne-blond version of Miss Crystal, possibly an older sister, has been in Phoenix the past two nights, working the bars Arriosto was known to frequent."

Carter's concentration was broken by a series of low-key hand signals from the Arab. The movements struck Carter as a combination of the hand language used by the deaf and the signs used by the independent bet takers at English racetracks.

"Something's just been cued. There's a scenario in progress," Carter said. "The PLO type just called the signals to set it in motion."

Hawk wasn't flapped. "Get to Phoenix. Find this Miss Crystal look-alike and the connection, if any, with LT. Check in from Toronto."

He ended the call as a well-orchestrated scenario unfolded in front of Carter:

Sichi's coffee was jostled by a woman dressed as an American tourist.

As Sichi rose to avoid being splattered, the "tourist" took his briefcase and tossed a small parcel at Sichi's feet.

A minivan paused at the curb and disgorged a group of Japanese tourists, who stepped goggle-eyed and bewildered into the bright afternoon sun.

The driver of the minivan got out, apparently to take a stretch. Without making a big thing about it, the guide, a man in ill-fitting gray pants and a baggy blazer, pushed some of the tourists out of the way. He produced a Ruger Mini 14 and began to blast Sichi, catching the terrorist completely by surprise.

Not to be outdone, the driver leveled a Tech-9 at the woman dressed as a tourist, and filled her chest with hollow tips that made a popping sound on contact.

By their subsequent posture and gestures, both men were now clearly providing cover and a means of getaway for the Arab, who moved quickly, picked up the attaché case Sichi had carried, and reached for the small parcel the lady "tourist" had tossed at Sichi's feet. The contents spilled and the Arab

went after them. Even from where he stood, Carter could tell
there were some first-rate uncut diamonds there.

It was all very neat and fast. The Japanese tourists, terri-
fied and screaming, scattered in all directions.

Abrams, the Mossad man, bolted the moment the shooting
began, scurrying across the busy street and disappearing into a
row of modernistic stores and boutiques located within a large
arcade.

The operation on Sichi had been so well orchestrated that
Carter couldn't even manage Hawk's request for a body
search. A number of individuals were already grouped around
Sichi and the woman. There was nothing for it now but to get
Abrams.

Moving quickly past the Place de l'Opéra and the pale pink
and green colors of the large nineteenth-century opera house
that always reminded Carter of a large, elaborately iced cake,
Lev Abrams pushed vigorously toward Boulevard de la Made-
leine, looking for all the world like a tourist on a brisk stroll.

Keeping a respectable distance between them, Carter
watched Abrams stop at a newsstand, using the opportunity to
see if there were any follow-up to the shooting he should be
aware of. The Mossad man continued toward Place de la Ma-
deleine and Carter formulated a plan, as intricate as a chess
gambit, that would allow him to intersect Abrams either on
the Boulevard des Capucines near the Olympia Music Hall, or
at nearby Fauchon, one of the most elegant stores for food and
cooking utensils in the sprawl of Paris.

Either site would be good. There was little chance of being
seen, little likelihood that what Carter planned would draw
more than passing attention from the Parisians.

After he'd bought a paper, Abrams began to pick up the
tempo of his stride. A short man with thinning sandy-red hair,
the Israeli appeared top-heavy. His shoulders were large and
square, his legs seemingly short and skinny. His sudden burst
of speed caused Carter to miss the connection he'd planned at
the Olympia.

Very well, Fauchon it was.

By some fast maneuvering through the back streets, Carter
arranged to pass Lev Abrams as he approached from the opposite direction. Drawing abreast of the Mossad operative,
Carter pretended to be interested in a display in a shop win-

dow. His hand moved casually to Wilhelmina. Luck was with him: there were only a handful of people on the street.

Carter showed the passing Abrams a glimpse of the Luger. The Mossad man stopped, perplexed and nervous.

"There's enough muzzle velocity here to leave a large hole at this range," Carter said in Hebrew. "That's surely enough reason for you to hold your hands out in front of you."

Abrams began to perspire. Being stopped like this so soon after the shooting was having an effect on his adrenals. "You're not Israeli," he said in English.

"Just wanted to make sure you understood me," Carter said, leading him to a roll-down metallic shop front of a brasserie that wouldn't be open until the evening. "Why were you following Sichi?"

The Mossad man shuddered involuntarily. "I don't know what you're talking about. If this is a holdup—"

"Not in the conventional sense," Carter said, casually replacing Wilhelmina in her holster. "I want information and since I don't have much time, I'm afraid I can't be overly polite about asking for it."

Abrams gave himself a few moments to recover from the chase, then lit a Gitane cigarette, blowing the pungent smoke out in a harsh rasp. "What do you want?"

"Why was the Mossad so interested in Sichi?"

Abrams glowered contempt at him. "I don't know what you're talking about."

"I don't have time for this, Abrams." The Israeli couldn't disguise the shock on his face at the sound of his name. "Just believe me when I tell you we're on the same side. If you share with me, I'll see that you get my findings on LT."

Abrams took a last drag on his cigarette and crushed the butt under his heel. The mention of the initials had hit a nerve. "Okay," he said at last. "Okay. Law of the lion."

"I lost you, Abrams," Carter said curtly.

"LT, you fool—*lex talionis*. Means law of the lion. Lex Talionis is a paramilitary goup wanting to be their own law."

"That's a new bunch, no?" Carter asked. "I never heard of them."

The little Mossad man nodded. "We've had only one report on them. From South Africa, of all places. Not from my sector. I don't like to work with those people, those Afrikaners.

I've been at this game long enough so that I don't have to take assignments relating to South Africa." His voice was edged with disgust.

Carter waited while the Mossad man lit another cigarette. "Sichi," he said. "Why were you on him?"

"To see if I could find out who he was dealing with. We had word he was betraying his people, the Red Brigade, by selling a cache of arms meant for them. He'd bought the arms in Marseille, and was here to sell them elsewhere."

"Any ideas?" Carter asked.

"You saw it go down. He had all the bills of lading and shipping materials in that briefcase. My guess is that Sichi was selling the arms to Lex Talionis."

"Who do you think it was who got him?"

"You must be new in this business if you don't recognize the Red Brigade," Abrams replied.

"I've been around long enough to recognize Abdul Samadhi from the PLO," Carter said, ignoring the jibe.

"Those two in the minivan were Red Brigade," Lev Abrams said, but Carter could see he was intrigued.

"You could be wrong about that," Carter suggested.

Abrams shrugged.

"There was a third spectator. Someone else was interested besides you and me," Carter said. Abrams blinked nervously. "In other words," Carter pressed, "your group hasn't a positive make on Abdul Samadhi."

Grudgingly, Abrams nodded. "Maybe he isn't important."

"Maybe," Carter agreed. "On the other hand, why would they let someone who wasn't experienced tail this operation?" He let that sink in, then pounced. "Why would they trust such a person to tail you?"

"You'll let me know if you find out anything?"

"Ah," Carter said, "I see I've raised some doubts in your mind. Yes, I believe in professional courtesy among colleagues. As soon as I get a line on Lex Talionis, I'll get you a briefing."

Carter exchanged contact information with the Mossad man, then hailed a taxi. He had an SST to catch.

# THREE

*Phoenix, Arizona*

Of all the spots on Hawk's list of places frequented by Arriosto, the Happy Breed seemed the most desperate to make a statement. It was in a glitzy, upscale neighborhood on Speedway. Lots of fern bars and expensive boutiques. The decor was high-tech. All the waitresses were at least six feet tall, their bodies pitched into the inviting postures spike heels forced on them. They wore black leotards, black mesh hose with seams, rhinestone chokers and anklets.

The bar menu was an expensive selection of imported beers, the house liquor the best brands. Appetizers were either Japanese or California nouvelle cuisine, and the cheapest mineral water on the menu was three dollars. The three-piece combo was all acoustic, the sounds a step away from Muzak. Even the cigarette smoke had a tinge of yuppie ambience and expensive conviviality.

Carter sat at the bar long enough to get the layout and see which of the waitresses best served his purpose. Dressed to fit in with the clientele, he wore a muted Madras shirt with long sleeves, light gray slacks, and plain black loafers. He finished his beer and approached a waitress whose movements were practiced and economical and who made no attempts to hide the traces of gray flecking her long dark hair. Her name tag read BOBBIE.

Carter extended a twenty. "I'd like to sit at your station the moment you've got an opening."

Bobbie's hazel eyes flickered over him like a laser verifying an American Express card. "Some men see my gray hair,

17

they think I'm desperate for favors," she said, ignoring the twenty. "All I do is serve drinks and food."

"That's exactly why I want to sit at your station." He dropped the twenty on her tray.

"I get it—you want me to scout for you. I don't do that, either."

Carter smiled. "Maybe I already understand that and want to drink alone."

Bobbie sighed and led Carter to a small table, then set a cocktail napkin before him. "If you'd wanted to drink alone, you wouldn't be here. I want to know what you expect for your twenty."

"Information," Carter said. He carefully showed Bobbie the photo of the Miss Crystal look-alike.

Bobbie narrowed her eyes. "Something isn't right about this photo."

Carter nodded. "I have that feeling too. If she comes in while I'm here, will you let me know?"

"You're a pro," Bobbie said. "Notice I didn't say cop. Okay. She comes in, I let you know."

Carter ordered another beer, lit a cigarette, and sat back, prepared for a long wait.

He tried the technique that had worked for him so many times: get a handle on someone's personality by absorbing as much background as possible and trying to fit the character to the background.

Apparently this place, the New Breed, had a style that touched the late Guillermo Arriosto, a man who might have been a relocated Argentine military man with a love of violence and a taste for young girls. A man who'd been content to let this part of the world see him as the Grinning Gaucho, a seller of four-wheel-drive, off-road, and specialty vehicles.

A few moments later Bobbie appeared, set his beer before him, and gave him change for the twenty. "Over there," she said, inclining her chin toward an area just to the right of the small bandstand. "In the green dress."

Carter looked at the change. "That was supposed to be for you."

"On the house," Bobbie said. "If you ever decide you're looking for something special and personal, you'll know where to find me." She gave a toss of that handsome, silver-streaked ebony hair and headed back to the bar.

No question about it, the woman in the green dress was the same one in Hawk's picture. Below medium height, a runner's rangy body, with hardly an ounce of spare fat. She wore a tight shiny green dress with a low scoop in front and an even more tantalizing vee in the back, crisscrossed with narrow laces. High heels with straps wrapped around the ankles emphasized her slender, muscular legs. Her hair was a champagne blond. Large, bright green earrings emphasized the angular shapeliness of her face. Carter looked closely, wondering what it was that he and Bobbie had seen in the photo that didn't ring true.

The blonde had some guy in tow, coming in and joining her a few moments after she'd been seated; he'd probably let her go in while he parked the car.

Watching her erect, graceful posture and the casual way she crossed her legs, Carter realized it had been a while since he'd had the luxury of some R & R. He even realized with a wry grin of amusement that his first response to the blonde had been frankly sensual instead of the professional assessment he'd trained himself to make.

Carter figured the blonde and the man had been out pub crawling. The man was starting to be deliberate and careful with his movements, suggesting he'd put away a few already. A beefy-looking guy, maybe mid-forties. A good, deep tan, pecs and biceps he was obviously vain about. Even so, Carter observed, he was starting to get a bit jowly and spreading at the gut.

Military type, Carter judged, but not out of any of the better academies. Maybe nothing more than ROTC at some lesser-rank college, possibly not even that—only a reservist somewhere. He had the look of discipline but not of class.

The blonde was working him leisurely, letting him get an occasional look when she leaned forward to get a cigarette, giving his hand a pat now and then, and even resting her hand on the guy's knee while the waitress was taking their order for drinks.

She was not matching him in drinks. Once, in the darkness, Carter saw her dump part of her glass and steer the guy's attention by crossing her legs and letting him return the compliment with a hand on her knee. This seemed to have the effect she was out to achieve. The guy now had both hands on her legs and leaned forward earnestly.

The blonde appeared to be thinking it over for a moment, then deftly moved his hands away, stood, and gathered her purse, cigarettes, and lighter.

She took a few steps and turned as if to see what was keeping the big guy. He was getting what he'd asked for, wasn't he? She even gave a saucy swing of her hips and he was up now, spilling his drink, calling for the check.

Carter, working from instinct and a healthy cynicism about ever letting down his guard, left through the front entrance and moved quickly down Speedway to the corner. He found an alley and stayed in the shadows, paralleling Speedway until he reached the parking lot of the New Breed. It was lit with low-wattage sodium vapor lamps, casting an eerie amber glow over the desert night. A heavy scent of jasmine came in on a gentle southern breeze, stirring the warm, heavy Phoenix night.

The parking lot was filled with BMWs, Mercedeses, an occasional Porsche or Lotus, and other examples of affluent taste. Carter stood in the shadows waiting, his keen senses alerting him, telling him not to relax.

At length the blonde and her date moved into the lot, his arm around her waist, and she appearing no longer casual or disinterested but instead caught up in her own eagerness.

The moment Carter's senses had been preparing him for came when the man tugged at the blonde. The Killmaster now knew that something was up and it wasn't what the blonde was expecting.

At first she thought he wanted an embrace, even presented herself to him, but he continued to tug at her arm. "Here's your car, right here," she said. She got no response from him and added, "That settles it—I'm driving."

"Let's go in this one instead," he said.

As the man spoke, Carter realized what was happening. To her credit, the blonde realized it a few moment later, after the man tugged at her once more.

"What is this?" she said.

The doors of a gray Mercedes opened and two other men appeared. Both military types. One was about six feet tall with a long scar on his left cheek, the other a sinewy black.

"Just get in," the blonde's date said, no longer the hard-drinking playboy. "No fuss, no muss. You understand?"

The blonde kicked out at her date, scoring a sharp jab along his right shin with the heel of her shoe.

Carter took that moment of action to make his own move. He sprang in front of the blonde's date and delivered a sharp kick to his left kneecap, sending him back against a car with a yowl.

"Hey, what's this? We got a helping hand for the lady," the black man said, and came at Carter with an overhand chop that was calculated to numb Carter's right arm and leave him vulnerable for a combination or a move from the man with the scar.

Carter wasn't in position to do more than roll away from the hand chop, which dealt him only a glancing blow. But Scarface, six feet and powerful, came at Carter like a street fighter, diving right at him for a tackle.

Knowing he was going to have to go down for a moment, Carter did a back roll, extended his feet, and took the tackler right in the gut. He sprang to his feet in time to see the blonde's date coming at him with a baton.

Carter poised, kick-turned, and used a Korean *gwan-kyo* maneuver, snapping the man's wrist with his foot. Now he spun around, slashed at the man with his left, pushed away his guard, and slammed his right fist into the side of his attacker's neck, felling him immediately.

The black man came at him, leaping from the hood of a car, catching Carter by the shoulders while his confederate approached with a large knife.

Carter smashed his left elbow into the black man's chest, wrenching his right arm free. With a quick twitch of his forearm muscle, Hugo, his razor-sharp stiletto, perfectly balanced and deadly, was in his right hand, ready for action. The Killmaster used a fast, underhanded snap toss, delivering Hugo right at the black man's carotid artery, where it was not likely to glance off any ribs.

The blonde watched with a gasp as the black man quickly lost the power even to try yanking Hugo from his neck.

That left only one assailant, who now kicked off his loafers and assumed a fighting stance Carter knew only too well.

Before Carter could get set, he felt a stinging jab under his left ear as Scarface, more lithe and faster than he appeared, reached him with a powerful Korean snap kick. Carter reeled and felt himself sinking. He tried to force concentration and move back, but a combination stomach kick and spin kick brought him down.

Scarface danced before him, moving in. "Not too well versed in the Korean style, eh, Killmaster?" His knee slammed against Carter's jaw, but Carter had opted to take the knee charge so that he could lash out at Scarface's thigh with the rigid side of his right hand.

Carter bought enough time to slow the next kick, get a purchase on Scarface's leg, and apply a wrenching twist.

Scarface lost his balance and made his position worse by trying to avoid landing on Carter.

His head still ringing but his senses clearing, Carter caught Scarface with a glancing side kick, spun, grabbed the man's arm, made a fulcrum with his own leg and gave him a compound fracture. His foot came down on the big man's ankle, producing a popping sound.

Scarface made a quick move with his left hand, and when Carter realized what the man had in mind, he kicked at the side of his opponent's face. For the first time in the encounter, Scarface smiled. "You *are* good, I'll say that for you. At least I lost to the best."

Carter turned from him and moved toward the girl.

"He's still moving!" she cried.

"Not for long," Carter said. "He had a poison ring and when he saw he was finished, he wouldn't risk the chance of talking." Carter turned back to Scarface, nudged him.

The poison was one of those quick-acting neural transmitters. The man was dead.

The blonde took a long look at Carter, then at the three inert forms of her attackers, and she began to tremble. For a moment she appeared vulnerable and naïve, a little girl caught wearing the clothes of a grown-up woman.

Watching her, Carter approached the black man, withdrew Hugo from his throat, then casually wiped the blade on the man's jacket.

"Lucky for me you were here," she said, taking several deep breaths and composing herself. Carter watched the trans-

formation back to mature womanhood as she faced him, aware
that her life had been very much at risk.

The blonde smiled at him, her face ripe with sensual challenge. Then she shook her head. "No, it wasn't luck at all,
was it?"

A half hour later they were in her rooms, a budget businessman's suite at the Sonesta on Indian School Road. Comfortable beds, large bathtubs, shower heads mounted far
enough up on the wall not to hit someone of Carter's size in
the chest, and even a Jacuzzi.

Carter was drinking beer. The blonde went for an occasional splash of cognac in her coffee. They sat on a large sofa,
close but not touching, aware of the intimacy and sensuality
building between them. Carter had seen that in the parking lot
and realized the blonde's reaction hadn't been fear at the
closeness of death, but rather a long moment of personal excitement at the closeness of complete involvement.

"You're a person who's been through a lot of political up-
heaval, or a professional," Carter said. "Which is it?"

The blonde sipped her coffee thoughtfully. "You must be in
there yourself to spot it so easily."

Aware that she was avoiding the question, Carter removed
the false back of his AXE-doctored Rolex and placed the tiny
microchip board near the telephone. No red warning light. He
did a quick sweep of the obvious places in the room. There
were no traces of a sophisticated bug that would pick up their
conversation.

Sitting next to her, he pressed on her background. "I'm
hoping you'll tell me why Guillermo Arriosto is so important
to you."

She took more brandy and asked for a cigarette. Even
though she was young, Carter could sense a growing patina of
the professional beginning to form around her. Under that,
there was something more. Pure, raw emotion. Some came to
this work through idealism, like Carter. Others came to it to
get even.

"I'm Susanna King. A few generations ago, the family
name hadn't been Anglicized. It was still Konig, but that was
before the family had to move. I was born in Buenos Aires,
but"—she gave a cynical laugh—"we didn't better ourselves

by much in the move from Germany to Argentina."

She paused to smoke, then went on with a story Carter had heard before with variations. The difficulties of a relocated life, the subtler and more obvious kinds of discrimination, and above all, the ruling military. "I don't think it will come as any surprise when I tell you we were subjected to massive repression."

Her family had not been especially political nor had she, but because of their background and their habits of reading and education, they asked the inevitable questions, especially when it had to do with questioning authority. Gradually, some of her family and friends began to become what was called *los Desaparacidos*—"the disappeared ones"—those who simply vanished without a trace.

Susanna had become politicized when Raoul, a young man she'd been seeing, suddenly disappeared. "He managed to get word back to me where he'd been taken and by whom."

Raoul was never seen or heard from again, but Susanna had joined an organization to help hide those who were considered prime targets for being disappeared, and to assist their families in getting news of them. It was there she'd learned of the man known as Guillermo Arriosto.

"That was not his real name, of course," she said with scorn. "He took that name when he came to this country, and he had the gall, the audacity, to call himself the Grinning Gaucho. The only thing he ever smiled about were his tortures and continuous human rights abuses. His real name was Hector Léon Cardenas. He was a ranking officer in the security police."

Susanna King had seen him a few times in parades and there were occasional photos of him in *La Prensa*. Even more important, Susanna and her associates began to read of Cardenas's activities in clearing out the university and other places of dissent. He openly boasted of his powers and the number of people he had turned back into patriotic, law-abiding citizens. "He was very proud of the training he was given by the Americans."

She shuddered at the memory and Carter had no doubt her experiences had been in many ways more demanding than the one she'd just gone through.

"There were a number of such types in the military," Susanna explained, "and we had to keep on the alert for all of them."

After the change of political power in Argentina, Susanna had come to the United States. "I remember a newspaper story telling of Cardenas's death. This was three years ago. As I read the account, I was filled with mixed emotions. On the one hand, the world was better off without such a man, but I remember feeling cheated that he escaped justice before the law."

Carter nodded. Those were his sentiments as well. "So you had every reason to believe him dead. What brought you back to his old haunts, going to the places he went?"

Susanna King watched Carter with care. "Someone close to me reported the unthinkable—the impossible. Hector Cardenas was still alive, brought to this country and given a new identity as some kind of political payoff."

"And you came to investigate by yourself."

Susanna King nodded soberly. Again she began to tremble. "I was very close, wasn't I?" she said.

"You were close to a number of things," Carter said. "You were on a valid lead to some of his associates. You were almost killed. Those men were professionals. One of them died rather than risk being in the position you were in."

Susanna King moved toward him. "This isn't my first brush with death," she said. "You saved me and now I wonder if you'd help me celebrate the fact that I'm still alive."

As she spoke, Carter realized how attracted he'd been to her, with her slim, graceful body, and her large, open eyes, and the incredible openness of her personality. He drew her to him, simply holding her for a long moment, actually feeling her releasing the tensions of the past hour.

Then she sighed agreeably and began to trace parts of his body with her cool, practiced fingertips.

At length they were completely comfortable, Susanna draping her legs over Carter's lap, and beginning to probe at him with tantalizing flickerings of her tongue and with a steady, dramatic use of her fingertips. Carter liked the game and quickly found places to apply alternating caresses and pressures. Deftly, quickly, he found her lips, covered her mouth with his, and found how sensitive she was along the insides of her elbows. He suspected she would be even more sensitive along the insides of her taut narrow thighs.

She was.

In a few short moments, Carter felt her arching, then tensing agreeably against him. "You're good at everything," she whispered with a soft moan. "We need to get out of our clothes and down to serious celebration."

While Susanna was in the shower, Carter did a quick security check on the door and all the windows. They were sealed in and safe for the time being. He found her purse and ran a quick check. Susanna King, if that's who she wanted to call herself, had the usual assortment of ID, and it all looked real enough.

Business could now be put on hold.

Carter began unbuttoning his shirt and removing Hugo's soft chamois sheath. The sound of the spraying water and the image of Susanna being drenched by it, the rivulets of water streaming between her breasts, caused a tremor of anticipation. Carefully removing his last bit of defense, Pierre, the tiny gas bomb taped to his inner thigh, Carter joined Susanna in the shower and offered to scrub her back—or do whatever else she desired.

# FOUR

Carter pulled the towel from Susanna King's hands, tossed it over the door of the stall shower, picked her up, and carried her into the bedroom.

She shifted her weight to accommodate being carried, placed her arms around his neck, and began biting playfully at his shoulders.

"Hey, what are you doing to me?" Carter chuckled.

"Nibbling. I want you to have souvenirs."

They were still partially wet when Carter landed them in a heap on the bed, but neither of them cared. Carter, who had been intrigued by the sight of her in the tight green dress, found her to be even more alluring in a state of nudity. Her body was frankly boyish and articulate with muscles, but the firmness and classic roundness of her breasts and the delicate, inviting sweep of her hips made Carter want to participate energetically in Susanna's celebration.

To his relief, she said nothing about his scars, the true campaign badges of Carter's career with AXE. Her fingers traced his thighs and back and she certainly took recognition of the places where bullets, knives, torture devices, and even shards of broken glass had pierced him and healed. Young as she was, she had a strong sense of herself that Carter liked and he knew that his impression of her, when he'd first seen her, was correct.

A man with Carter's life-style had to be selective and make every moment count. There was the more recreational sex attraction, which was fine for recharging the senses. There was also the creative sexual attraction, which touched deeply

27

and made life seem valuable. Susanna King was certainly the more creative type.

Carter began kissing her damp shoulders and breasts, giving himself over to the creative possibilities.

Susanna set about giving him a more agreeable assortment of kisses down his chest and belly, and soon Carter began to realize how caught up in her sensuality she was. He took the initiative again and quickly brought her to the point where she was moving against him, arching and thrusting, her strong hands clutching his shoulders. "Not that way," she pleaded. "Not now. Join me. Be with me. Hold me." But Carter persisted and soon her body twitched again involuntarily with galvanic pleasure.

Carter could feel her surrender herself to their lovemaking, and the knowledge that she was most likely someone and something other than what she had represented herself to be impressed him as he finally joined their bodies.

If she was a professional, her trust was either touching or foolish.

All thought of that quickly faded.

Susanna brought an intensity and energy to their lovemaking that quickly took over. Gently surrendering himself to it, Carter smiled and supposed it was only fair after what he'd done to her.

Carter was awakened by the sound of the telephone. She'd made no attempt at subterfuge or stealth, and when she saw Carter's eyes opening, she covered the mouthpiece and said, "Does lovemaking give you an appetite?"

"Invariably," Carter said.

Susanna started to order, but Carter took the phone from her and ordered in Spanish a number of Mexican dishes including the piquant green chili so famous in central and southern Arizona.

While they were waiting for the order to be brought, Carter again checked the door, the hallway, and the windows. For good measure, he ran another check on the phone. "Equipment is so sophisticated these days, they don't even have to be in the room to turn the phone into a microphone."

Susanna nodded, propped herself up on one elbow, and eyed Carter speculatively. "I'm having a very good time with you," she said, "and I'm probably a little in love with you, but I happen to be a practical and realistic sort and so I wonder if we could have the rest of the day together."

"How about until breakfast, tomorrow morning?" Carter countered.

"I think I am in love with you," Susanna King said. "But only until breakfast."

Using some of Susanna's things, Carter took a quick shave and by the time he'd finished, room service arrived with what they both agreed was enough food and drink to last them until tomorrow morning.

Wheeling the serving dolly over to the side of the bed, Carter produced dishes and glasses. They ate and drank, unselfconscious about being naked, their hands meeting occasionally, their eyes filled with the admiration of each other and the knowledge of what was still before them.

Carter decided it was best to get business out of the way. He still had something to say to her and now seemed the proper time.

"I've come to the conclusion that Hector Cardenas was not the only one with a laundered identity," he said.

While Susanna was spooning generous gobs of the green chili over her *huevos rancheros*, Carter went to his wallet and retrieved the photo of Miss Crystal left for him in the private jet that took him from Toronto to Phoenix.

"Anyone you know?" he asked.

To her credit, Susanna didn't miss a beat and kept right on eating. "I told you that someone close to me began to suspect. It was my younger sister, Crystal."

"And now you've decided to find out for yourself?" He sat down on the edge of the bed, took the fork from her hand, and set it on her plate. Taking both her hands in his, the Killmaster said, "It's much more plausible that you're a brunette under that blond dye job, and that you used a product called eye collagen along with another formula, Retin A, available from the more enlightened dermatologists. You were able to make yourself look quite a bit younger, and judging from the outfit you wore in this photo, you were able to make yourself appear to be the type that so excited Guillermo Arriosto, alias Hector Cardenas."

Susanna King pulled her hands free and began eating again.

"Was it indeed Cardenas at Covington?"

"Yes," she said matter-of-factly, looking now for some jam made from the nopal cactus. "From the things he asked me to do—the sexual things—and all the other similarities, I concluded it was him."

"Concluded?" Carter said.

"But not quite positive." She stopped chewing, paused reflectively, and turned to face Carter. "I-I wanted to be positive, but something wasn't quite right. There were striking similarities and yet there were differences—"

"What kind of differences?"

"Appearance. Cardenas was known to have scars about his lower torso. He liked it when—he asked me to put on a French maid's costume and to pretend I was angry with him and to spank him. I was told this had left many scars from previous times."

Susanna poured them both coffee and sipped hers slowly. "He had a younger face than I expected, and one of my reports said his eyes were rather close together."

"Crossed?"

"No, not that way, simply the effect of a smaller head. But so many other things checked out. I have to conclude that it was Cardenas. I reported to my people that it was indeed Cardenas."

"And after the body was stolen, your people suspected it had something to do with the CIA."

She nodded guilelessly.

Carter trusted her. "Then you were instructed to come here to Phoenix and, in the role of Miss Crystal's older sister, see if you couldn't pick up any fresh leads."

Susanna nodded again. "See if I could get any leads on the others who were with him at Covington. See if there were any other leads or connections here."

"My guess," Carter said, "would be that you told me the truth about your background in Argentina, and the ones you now refer to as your people are, in fact, the Mossad."

Susanna King watched him thoughtfully, then broke into a smile. "You won't tell them about *this*, will you?" she said, picking up a large shrimp and dipping it into a small container of mustard, then slowly placing the shrimp in her mouth.

"Ah, of course," Carter said with a laugh. "Shrimp aren't kosher."

"But it is very, very good, Mr. Killmaster from AXE."

"Another of your conclusions?" Carter said.

"Makes sense. The guy in the parking lot called you Killmaster, and you're certainly better than any FBI or CIA operative I've ever seen. Also, when I came here, I was told the names of all the FBI and CIA people in the area. Mostly the FBI agents who are here all the time and one CIA man named Zachary. For you to have missed our surveillance, you must have come in by private sources."

"What's your real name?"

She shook her head. "You already know enough about me. Why would you care about that?"

"I want to call you by your real name while we're making love," Carter said.

"It's lucky for me and my career that I don't go for everyone the way I do for you. All right, my name is Rachel. Rachel Porat. I'll be twenty-four in four months. I really am from Argentina, and I went with the Mossad because I'm more or less in sympathy, and they aren't in a position to turn down likely operatives because of something as mundane as age."

"Care to tell me your real interest in Cardenas?"

She hesitated. "The part about his causing some of my family and friends to disappear is true. From that sense, it was purely a bonus that I'd known about him as he really was. We have him connected with attempts to start dealing in weapons and ammunition. He was specifically interested in Belgian FN-FALs and if not those, then AK-47s."

"He was certainly after good stuff," Carter acknowledged.

"He was also after the H & K 91."

Carter knitted his brow. "That fires a .762 NATO round. His tastes in guns are rather interesting."

"Our people link him with another man who greatly interests us, a man who is also interested in guns and ammunition —Piet Bezeidenhout."

"The head of the South African diamond cartel security police?"

"That's the one. My immediate superior considers him one

of the most dangerous and venal men in the security profession today."

Carter felt his spine begin to prickle. He'd heard of Bezeidenhout's activities in and out of South Africa. An idea began to formulate. "Do the initials *LT* mean anything to you?"

"Lammed tav?" The woman who was Rachel Porat shrugged noncommittally.

Carter grabbed her shoulders. "Don't play games with me, Rachel. I don't mean Hebrew letters. I mean English ones, *L* and *T*."

She pulled away from his grip, and stood up. Vulnerable in her nakedness and desire, but torn by something deep inside. Carter had touched a nerve.

"Dammit, Carter, I've given you enough. Can't we just—"

"No," Carter snapped, "we can't. *LT* could be something of momentous proportions. If you know anything, you should share."

"Find your own leads," she said angrily. "We have to work hard for what we get, and now, all of a sudden, everyone thinks we're world-class heavies."

"Are you?" Carter asked.

"What do you think?"

Carter shook his head. "It doesn't matter what I think. I know who pays my rent and I know how far I'm willing to go to earn my pay. What about you?"

"*LT* is top-echelon stuff for us. If we develop our investigations and find out we were right, we can go in and stop it, and suddenly we're looking good again because we've removed something dangerous.Something potentially risky here in America and Canada. Then the rest of the world owes us. It's not my idea of how to do business, but in case you hadn't noticed, we're not exactly winning popularity contests these days."

"When you say 'go in,' you mean like at Entebbe?"

"I was only a kid then, Carter. I wasn't with them."

The Killmaster said nothing, stood, and lit a cigarette. He took a few drags, organizing his thoughts, then looked her in the eye.

"I've got this assignment too, Rachel, and I mean to develop it until I know what it is. If it's something as big as it looks, we'll have to take steps to stop it."

Rachel Porat made a snicker of distaste. "One stubborn American senator could slow down the entire procedure with delays and tin cans tied to the tail. One ambitious CIA operative, looking for name and glory, could ruin it."

"My organization has its own mandates, but it still respects the democratic process. If you give me something of value, I can promise you a return if I develop anything from your lead."

Rachel shook her head bitterly. "It becomes so damned political, Carter. Suppose you think there's nothing in it? Suppose we do?"

"Look, Rachel, I know what you're saying. But my group doesn't have to protect people. Very few persons know about us—the president and a few key others. Our size is strictly limited. There's no way we can get out of hand or lose touch with reality. In a very real sense, we're above politics."

"I'm going to trust you, Carter, because you saved my life, and because your being here isn't any accident."

"I think," Carter said, "you're doing the right thing."

Rachel Porat began to walk about the room, filled with the tenseness of her decision. After a minute or two she sat next to him and made eye contact all the while she spoke.

She might have been young and vulnerable, but she had the hard center necessary to be a good agent. It became clear to Carter that the accident of Rachel's Argentine background and her knowledge of Cardenas had influenced the higher echelons of the Mossad to let her in on more than they had Abrams, the operative running in Paris.

The Mossad had reason to believe Lex Talionis, whatever its goals were, was growing, gaining momentum and followers. They weren't clear where the money was coming from, but it was apparently well financed.

"Does the name Abdul Samadhi mean anything to you?"

Rachel Porat frowned. "Little cast-eyed PLO pig with a cleft chin trying to run up a reputation for himself."

Carter motioned for her to continue.

What came out was a series of anomalies—apparent or suspected dealings between persons who were either natural enemies or close to it. "As it was, I can tell you the names of three men who spent time with Cardenas in the meetings he held at Covington." Purposefully, she gave Carter some names of members of the notorious *tonton macoute* secret police from the deposed "Baby Doc" Duvalier regime, a former member of Ferdinand Marcos's staff, and an ardent white supremacist from Idaho.

"You know for a fact they were there?"

Rachel nodded. "I have the names of others who met with him, but I will end this conversation and all our covenants if you push me on these. Two of them we want, one of them *I* want."

"I understand," Carter said.

She smiled, relieved. "In that case, there is a name I will give you, because I don't think I'm going to be able to get to Mexico City just yet."

"You're determined to work these people Cardenas met with?"

"And his contacts here. Cardenas was planning something big, big enough to betray the people who laundered him and brought him in."

Maybe not betray them, Carter thought, but he said nothing. He waited while Rachel Porat began to describe and lead up to the contact in Mexico City.

Carter had to stop her. "Why are you hesitating like this?"

"Because, damn you, I'm jealous." Then she went on to explain why. "The person I'm sending you to, Margo Huerta, is a fascinating woman. She's tall, good-looking, sensual. She's an artist who is well respected, and she has great passions for everything in life. I know what will happen when she sees you." While she went on describing Margo Huerta, Rachel lapsed into the formalized, stilted method of reporting that characterized so many police, security, and political organizations.

"Subject is known to have significant contacts with liberal fund-raising groups and is thought to have funneled funds for indigenous tribespeople and nationalist fighters involved in armed conflicts with American- and Soviet-sponsored military groups." While Rachel Porat spoke, Carter had to muster all his control not to erupt into a large grin, but he was successful at keeping a poker face.

Rachel's description was professional enough, although she did manage a few catty digs.

When she finished talking, she looked at her watch. They

had sixteen hours left—sixteen hours for Rachel Porat to work out her jealousy in ways that would give Nick Carter something to think about when he was in Mexico City. "Come here," she said. "I'm going to make sure you remember me."

Carter eased out of Rachel's room while she slept. It was not an easy decision to make. Theoretically he was still on schedule, and as Rachel lay there, her hair spilling over the pillow, her body warm and inviting, he was tempted to wake her up for a proper farewell.

But Carter sighed, went to the door, and left. He used the taxi trip to Phoenix International Airport to set the complex skein of events in perspective. He had time to put in a call to Hawk and for a barbershop shave and massage before his flight to Mexico City boarded.

"I imagine your interview with Miss Crystal was productive," Hawk said, and Carter could hear the sucking and puffing of smoke as well as Hawk's ironic bite.

Hawk listened carefully as Carter went through the details. "No question about it, Nick. This is a profitable line of enquiry. While you were digging up your details, we got a few of our own. We had to twist a few arms, and the CIA bloody well yowled when I gave them a quid pro quo. They hadn't known one of their boys had been doubled by the Cubans. Here's what it amounts to."

He went on to report that Guy Prentiss had been in Mexico City shortly before his death, trying to contact old intelligence sources, especially a rare book dealer named Norman Sasner. "Prentiss was desperately trying to get word through that he was on to something."

"Did that have any effect?"

"You know the bureaucratic maze, Nick. CIA and State took notice, but in all cases, they discounted his reliability and placed the material in a file where it will stay until they either get confirmation or decide it isn't worth pursuit."

There was a long pause and Carter could hear the TV monitors in the background. A private teletype began to clatter, bringing forth fresh, reliable information from somewhere in the world.

"We're most interested in the participation of this Bezeidenhout fellow. Pursue that. Find him if you can. See if you can discover what he's up to. Is this something he's doing for the South African diamond cartel?"

"Could it be something he's working on independently, sir?"

"Good question. Find out. We need to know that. Those diamond security police pay their operatives well, but they brook no nonsense. If a man is caught with even the suspicion of an unsavory deal, there are severe reprisals."

Hawk paused to let that sink in.

"See if you can get any fresh material from the sources our colleagues at the Agency and State missed," he continued. "Go to Mexico City and keep in touch, especially if you land anyone who is a member of this Lex Talionis."

"I'll see if I can get you some Cuban cigars," Carter said.

"Don't bother," Hawk growled, but not without regard.

# FIVE

Several noted commentators have projected that the huge sprawl of Mexico City would be the largest metropolitan area in the world by the end of the century. There were already twenty-eight million people living in varying degrees of opulence or poverty, depending on where you drew the line between luxury suites and packing crates. Probably another two or three million more than that if you remember that census programs begin to lose their accuracy as you move closer to the pockets where the poor and the dispossessed try to eke out a living.

As far as Carter was concerned, Mexico City already was the largest, measurably larger since his last visit a few years earlier. A heavy layer of smog pressed down, amplified by the rattle and clatter of slow-moving streams of cars and trucks without mufflers and, even worse, by too many smoke-belching diesel-powered vehicles.

The usual afternoon cloudburst fell within minutes of four o'clock, and a light breeze promised some relief from the day's heat, but at an altitude of seven thousand feet, it would take something more forceful to clean out the smog. So it was clear that while you were here, there were other things on your mind besides clean air: a twenty-four-hour-a-day lifestyle, some of the most beautiful women in the world, some great restaurants, first-rate museums, top performances in every kind of music, some of the finest minds in the world today as well as some of the most devious, the opportunity to cut deals with the wealthy and the needy from all over the world.

Carter went to a favorite café, the Tupinamba, home of the

bullfight crowd. He washed down a light lunch of lamb shank and green peas with two bottles of Carta Blanca pilsner, then made it official that he was back in Mexico by having a syrupy Mexican coffee, half-and-half with steamed milk.

Checking the list of his contacts, he decided on the Plaza Florencia as his hotel. Just off Mexico City's main avenue, Paseo de la Reforma, it was convenient to the Zona Rosa, the so-called Pink Zone that reminded Carter in many ways of the Georgetown area of Washington, D.C. In both places, the shops, galleries, restaurants, and bistros were definitely upscale.

From the Plaza Florencia, Carter could pursue his meeting with Margo Huerta, the artist Rachel Porat had told him about. It was convenient as well to the rare book dealer, Norman Sasner. Apparently desperate, Prentiss had tried to contact any legitimate source before his driving urge to tell what he'd known about Lex Talionis had brought him and the CIA man, Merton, violent death. He'd also be within blocks of a café where he could either find or make contact with Chepe Muñoz, another person Prentiss was known to have contacted.

Chepe Muñoz was apparently another kettle of fish altogether, and Carter was looking forward to meeting him. Nominally tied in with the opposition, Muñoz was supposed to be a bright, quick man who always put human concerns and ideals above political jargon.

Margo Huerta was immediately responsive to Carter's call, but told him she was working on a large piece—a mural— and couldn't see him until later in the evening. Rachel's jealousy had served to give the Killmaster advance notice. He was certain he caught a strong impression of the artist's sensuality even over the phone.

Carter decided to try Norman Sasner. Sasner ran his business on Isobel la Católica, a bit of a walk, but one that would literally help Carter get his Mexico City legs and lungs by helping him adjust to exercise at the higher altitude. A rare book shop made a perfect blind for processing information, investigating local activities, and allowing other informants to appear without fear of creating suspicion. A rare book store could be closed for long hours or days on end without creating suspicion.

The Killmaster strolled leisurely along Juarez until it

turned into Francisco Madero. Then he turned right for a block on Bolivar and found what he was looking for just below the intersection of 16 de Septiembre and Isobel la Católica.

In a concrete building from the 1920s, Norman Sasner, Rare Books, was on the second floor, above a watch repair and a small cafeteria where the customers were given large flour tortillas instead of trays, and were charged by the serving ladle of food plopped on that large expanse of edible container. The odors of fish, chiles, onions, and grilling marinated meats made Carter wish he hadn't eaten so well at Tupinamba.

The stairway was hewn from dark mahogany planks that had done well over the years. Mounting the steep incline, Carter was passed by three men, one of whom hesitated for a moment, as though in recognition.

Through the smells of middle-class cooking, Carter got another odor and suddenly the picture became complete for him.

These guys were pros and something had just gone down.

Carter caught a whiff of burning cordite.

A gun had been discharged recently.

The man who'd hesitated very probably had recognized Carter—or suspected him of being someone on the other side.

Carter spun around and tripped the second of the three men, a nondescript sort in a three-piece suit. The one who had hesitated turned, but before he could free his Ruger Mini-14, Carter had Hugo out, aimed, and thrown. The man smiled benignly as Hugo dug into him with a pocking sound. Only then did Carter realize the man wore a bulletproof vest. Hugo may have drawn blood, but any real damage was negligible.

The Ruger was leveled right at Carter, who had no option now but to push off the stairway and dive at his attacker. A roar of discharging gun tore a furrow in the skin of Carter's shoulder as the two men collided on the stairway.

The Killmaster's momentum carried him into the man with the Ruger and also caused a massive collision with the nondescript confederate. A raking kick to the man's shin had him doubled up with pain. The gun was leveled at Carter again. He rolled to get into position, used both hands to push himself off a stair, and with his right foot knocked the gun from his assailant's hand. It went skittering down the stairs.

The assailant let out a yell more in frustration than pain, and the one whose shin Carter had scored was yelling in frustration of his own to the third man, "Get him, dammit!"

The third man came at Carter with the butt of his palm. Carter found a quick stance of balance, caught the man's slicing palm, used the descending arm as a fulcrum, and caused him to go reeling, off-balance, tumbling down the rest of the stairs.

The largest of the group, the one who'd had the gun, came at Carter and shot a kick at his knee.

Carter knew he'd have to take it, but he also knew he could minimize the effects by dropping into a roll.

He got a hand on his attacker's handmade shoe and yanked.

The big guy swore again, went over backward, and landed on his advancing confederate.

They pushed away from each other, the frustration starting to get to them.

Carter made a lunge for Hugo and used an underhanded toss as the big guy reached for his Ruger. Hugo pinned him and he let out a yowl. "Son of a bitch!" he shouted, yanking Hugo out of his hand. "I'll get you!"

Carter motioned him on with a come-hither gesture of both hands. The big man said to his confederates, "Come on, let's get him!"

They looked at him uneasily.

Grinning wickedly, Carter did a jump-kick turn, catching the one at the farthest end right at the kneecap. The pain was excruciating.

Clutching his knee, he went rolling down the steps to yet another kind of pain.

Suddenly Carter heard the wail of a siren. It was time to get out of there.

The men looked at each other and swore with disgust. There were three of them and they couldn't take Carter.

Hugo was tossed scornfully at Carter's feet.

The three men scurried off, limping, down 16 de Septiembre. Carter decided there was nothing to be gained from chasing them. Chances of getting useful information were better inside.

Whether the siren was in response to what they'd done up

in Sasner's office or not, Carter knew he didn't have much time.

He headed up the stairs into the rare book dealer's offices, knowing in advance what he would find.

The interior was one large room, wall-to-wall books with the exception of a small alcove that was dominated by a large colonial-style desk and a Bank of England chair. A small room off to the side had packing and shipping equipment, plus a long worktable with large stacks of catalogues and the life-blood of the rare book business, the magazine Antiquarian Bookman.

If Sasner's rare book business had been set up as a blind, it had at least been done by someone who had a certain amount of taste and knowledge. There were a number of first editions by Latin American authors and many fine volumes by European and American writers.

On the far wall were some of the more cosmetic titles in the rare book business, old atlases, eighteenth-century maritime charts, and a number of beautiful leather-bound sets on colonial Mexico.

Sasner was clearly a man who had thrived on an image of himself. A dapper little man with a double-breasted blazer sporting a large crest, an RAF necktie, and brown suede wing tips, he'd sat at his large desk, his corpse now driven back, arms splayed by the muzzle velocity of the two bullets he'd taken. One shot had blasted him in the throat, another in the heart.

Carter took in the cruel reality of death. He'd seen it hundreds of times. A person's dignity gone in that last moment, leaving a picture that was actually a parody of the image the victim had tried to maintain in life. Here, Norman Sasner, in death, had his secret revealed. The force of the bullets that had killed him had also dislodged a rather complex toupee. Nevertheless, Sasner had managed to do what Carter had expected. By dipping his neatly manicured index finger into a large silver ink pot, Norman Sasner had managed to leave a clue: *LT*.

Carter looked quickly about the desk for anything that looked like a note or dispatch Sasner might have thought to pass on to his CIA people. There was no time for a comprehensive search.

He glanced around the desk area, trying to look for anomalies. There was a stack of the *Manchester Guardian*, but it quickly became apparent to Carter that Sasner's interest in this rather political newspaper was the reporting of English soccer league scores. The Killmaster also noticed an invitation to a poetry reading at the university and a tiny stack of *Soldier of Fortune* magazines, but nothing that seemed an obvious piece of what was growing to be a vexing puzzle.

He decided to get out of there and take care of his shoulder.

He removed his sports jacket, draped it over the shoulder with the wound, and quickly found a taxi on Isobel la Católica, giving directions for a small, discreet emergency hospital not far away on Calle Mesones.

Whoever they were, Lex Talionis certainly had some organizational claws and were now trying to cover their tracks. Even more important, Carter realized, they were on to him and his interest in them.

"Always intriguing problems you bring me, Carter." Dr. Hakluyt, a resident of Mexico for more than forty years, still retained the speech patterns and metallic pronunciation of his native Europe.

A shaggy, Falstaffian man with curly graying hair, he regarded the Killmaster now as Carter lay, facedown, on a padded table, bathed in powerful mercury vapor light. "Last time you were here, you bring me the interesting problem of sutureless procedure. Now I think there is no way we are going to avoid some stitches."

Carter lay quietly, watching Hakluyt's assistant, a tall, striking woman with wide, high cheekbones and the dark hair and eyes that spoke so eloquently of her Indian ancestry. She seemed aware of Carter's interest, and as Hakluyt stitched the crease on Carter's shoulder, she let her gaze, shadowy with obsidian mystery, dance across his face. Her gaze was direct and filled with challenge—until she suddenly gave way to a grin.

"Interesting man," she said in Spanish to the doctor. "He brings us bullet wounds and hickeys."

"I assure you I favor the hickeys," Carter said in the musical Spanish of the capital city.

The nurse blushed, but her gaze remained steady.

Half an hour later, bandaged, given a handful of pills for pain and antibiotics, Carter was paying his tab.

"It is I who should pay you," Hakluyt said. "Such challenging problems you bring me, Carter. Far be it for me to wish you ill, but I do look forward to your visits. Last time it was the abdominal wall. This time the bullet is creasing your upper muscle sheath."

The old doctor's gruffness had a layer of paternalistic concern in it, reminding Carter of David Hawk. "You are in good condition. Your wound will knit very well and you will have full use of the shoulder, that is if you do not aggravate it for some weeks."

Carter nodded thoughtfully. "Tell me, Doctor, how completely is it possible to surgically change the human appearance?"

"Ah, a most intriguing question for one of your apparent profession. I tell you, Carter, if you could check in here and give me six weeks—even as few as four weeks—I could do things with your nose, literally lower your ears, perhaps even give you higher cheekbones like those you admire on my surgical nurse."

"I didn't mean for me," Carter said. "I mean in general."

"There are some gifted reconstructive surgeons, especially in your country." Hakluyt seemed to be sorting through a mental list. "One of the best at cosmetic reconstruction is Charles Smith. Truly gifted, but equally eccentric. I have seen him repair radial blowouts and maxillofacial traumas that would make you wince when you saw pictures of the original state. Very good with birth defects and traumas. You know, burns, explosions, violent impact."

Dr. Hakluyt spread his knobby hands. "Yes, Carter, if I grasp your meaning, it is possible to take an individual and in the hands of a gifted plastic surgeon, render him or her all but unrecognizable even to intimates."

Carter caught a cab and directed it to the Zona Rosa, where he made for the Palacio de Hierro on Durango, one of the best department stores in the city. He studied the rack of sports jackets, settled on a muted silk weave with flecks of blue and green, then found a blue cotton shirt. At the toiletries counter, he splashed himself with Jean-Marie Farina from Roger & Gallet, and set out to walk the six blocks to Bucareli, where Margo Huerta had her studio and living quarters.

"I apologize for running late," Margo Huerta said, standing back to regard a long panel of Masonite board, largely covered with a bright, angular, and forceful mural of entire families sleeping at a railroad station. "But as you can see, I work big, and when I get involved with something, I lose track of the time."

Watching her, Carter sipped the strong Mexican coffee she'd given him. Her studio was a large, narrow arrangement, running nearly a hundred and fifty feet. Walls had once divided her work area into two, perhaps three smaller studios. A large bank of custom windows caught a diamond-hard northern light. Sketches, unframed larger works, and several more conventional paintings were hung from the walls or leaned haphazardly against any handy surface. From two large speakers, strategically mounted to provide maximum stereophonic effect, came the clean, precise lines of one of Bach's Brandenberg Concertos, and as the selection came to an end, the distinctive, low-key voice of one of the XELA-FM announcers.

Herself a large, dark, flamboyant woman with an expressive face and as yet no need for a bra, Margo Huerta favored the bright colors of acrylic, drippings of which spattered the floors and her Levi's. There were several places on the unfinished wooden floor where there appeared to be violent crosshatchings made by a knife. Carter realized that Margo Huerta took a direct approach to cutting canvas or mounting her work, preferring the floor to a worktable.

"If you can handle my working and not fawning all over you, we can talk," Margo said. "Some men find that very threatening, especially you guys. We call you *norteños*. You call yourself Americans. That's a lot of snobbery, you know. We're all Americans."

"What I'm trying to figure is where that accent of yours comes from," Carter ventured.

"Oh, I make no bones about it," Margo said, beginning work on a large, menacing figure. "I got some good education in your country. A few of your so-called liberal arts colleges in the South want to prove they're right for government grants, so they put on the big search for what they like to call minority women."

Margo daubed fiercely at the mural, the figure taking on the identity of a *federale*, a Mexican federal cop, waving a riot stick. Just short of six feet tall, she nevertheless chose to work in high heels. The top of her torso was barely covered with a paint-stained sleeveless sweatshirt, a souvenir of a long-forgotten Grateful Dead concert. Her long, ebony hair was tied in a complex knot, held in place with a bright pink scarf, giving a sensual accent to her café-au-lait skin.

"What they meant by minority women was anyone who didn't have blond hair, blue eyes, and creamy white skin," Margo Huerta said with a hoot of disdain.

Carter let her tell her own story, which she did directly enough. The child of a well-to-do family, Margo Huerta had been polite and mannered until her school experiences in the U.S. Her drawings, technically brilliant, were largely of flowers, seascapes, animals. "All the safe stuff, you know. But none of that was making me happy."

At length she'd begun doing larger works, commemorating events of Mexican history. "Would you believe it, Carter? All of a sudden that made me controversial. A lot of people don't want to see their own history. Suddenly I had a purpose, and I've been at it ever since. I get top prices for this stuff, Carter. Can you believe it?"

"No question about it," Carter said, pouring himself more coffee. "Your work is museum quality."

"Hah!" she said, spinning around, challenging him. "What do you know of museums? What was the last one you were in?"

"As a matter of fact, the Pompidou in Paris was the last one, earlier this week. And a short while before that, the Top-kapi in Istanbul."

Margo Huerta was impressed. "Pretty good for a CIA man."

"I think that is what is meant as a backhanded compliment," Carter said, "but I'm not CIA. Nothing like that."

"State Department? You aren't one of those little Ivy League career pantywaists?"

Smiling, Carter shook his head.

"And Rachel has sent you to me. You must be something in the profession."

Carter lit one of his cigarettes. "Let's stop trying to qualify each other and see what you can tell me about Lex Talionis."

"If you know about that, Carter, you are no mere art lover." She laughed at her own irony, plunked the three brushes she'd been using into a pot of solvent, and approached Carter, reminding him of a stately flamenco dancer. "What did Rachel tell you about me?"

"She told me she was jealous of your beauty."

"So that's how you got where you are. You made her fall in love with you."

"Only for a day," Carter said. "We're all too grown up for the other."

Still circling him, Margo Huerta moved closer, watching him with renewed interest and challenge. She took the remains of Carter's cigarette from him and smoked it for a moment. "Tell me, Carter, do you think I will fall in love with you for a day?"

Carter smiled. "I think I would be very pleased if you did. But whether that happens or not, I still need to talk about Lex Talionis." He decided to risk telling her about Norman Sasner.

"He was a great fool," Margo said, leading Carter over to an antique horsehair sofa, a classic analyst's couch. "I am not an official member of the intelligence community. My interests are in causes and I know activist sorts, so when I tell you it was open knowledge that he passed information to the CIA, you will get my point. If I knew, imagine what the professionals know. No descretion."

"Apparently he was well regarded at one time, and had good connections," Carter ventured.

"But he became caught up in the game and lost all sense of discretion."

Nick Carter went on to fill her in on the background of Prentiss, then sketched in his knowledge of Hector Cardenas and the mission Rachel Porat was on, resolving that he would tell no more unless he got a significant lead from Margo.

She sensed his caution.

"I tell you, Carter, I'm beginning to respect the way you work." She sighed as if clearing away any last-minute doubts about him. "Even if I were foolish enough to ask you for some identification, you would probably produce something that would look official and convincing and be completely worthless."

Carter smiled, and reached for his wallet.

"All right," she said. "I'll go for the big casino. If you qualify, we proceed. If not, well, perhaps we have dinner and fall in love for a day, and I finish my mural and you go back to school."

She asked for and lit another of Carter's cigarettes. "Does it mean anything to you that Bezeidenhout is at this very moment in Mexico? Only this week, he was here in the city, hosting a group of associates."

Carter did a quick scan of the leads he had. "Circumstantially, at least, it appears that Piet Bezeidenhout has defected from the security police and he may have burned them for several million in diamonds. He is probably a key player in the Lex Talionis organization."

Even as he spoke, an additional connection came through to him. "It also seems that Piet Bezeidenhout was having the same kind of meetings here in Mexico City that Hector Cardenas was having in Covington, Kentucky. He was making presentations and trying to interest potential backers."

Margo Huerta's eyes lit with admiration. "You are, as they say, a heavy hitter, Carter. Okay. We go on from here. I think we are going to get you somewhere and once we get there, not have to stop and check in with Daddy every time you need to make a decision." She rose, looking triumphant, moved to a small closet, and disappeared into it. Carter could hear the sounds of clothes hangers moving over a rack. Moments later, Margo emerged, looking a bit more formal from the top up. The cut-off sweatshirt had been replaced by a bright red silk blouse, a matching scarf, and a well-worn denim jacket. Margo looked as if she were off to a gallery opening or an evening of pub crawling. Carter began to get a suspicious, prickly feeling about her.

"Come on, Carter. We're off. I'll bet your people didn't give you anything about Chepe Muñoz, eh? Well, he's someone your boy, Prentiss, was in contact with. Knows his way around the CIA and the Cubans."

Carter, of course, had been briefed on Muñoz, but he saw no reason to tell Margo Huerta that, since his suspicions of her were beginning to mount.

"We'll take my car," she said.

Margo locked up carefully, made sure the dead bolt on the large door to her studio engaged, then pulled a small chain security door into position and locked it.

As they started down the steps toward the rear garage, Carter began to realize why he'd been suspicious. There were five of them, arranged in two groups so that on first look it would appear to be a group of garage mechanics talking or, even more innocently, a bunch of teenagers. They were all relatively short and wiry.

Carter assessed them quickly.

They were good with feet, hands, or weapons.

They were lethal and ready.

# SIX

Carter knew that in Mexico you get great clues about people by the shoes they wear. The affluent wore handmade shoes or high-fashion brands. A large number of Mexican youths wore running or sports shoes; in some cases, a pair of cheap soccer shoes was the only pair the individual owned.

All five of the crew that waited for them wore new, expensive Nikes. Their trousers, although khakis, had the unmistakable look of being professionally pressed.

They dispersed and moved with strategic expertise, like dancers in some deadly ballet.

Carter saw immediately that what he'd mistaken for youth in the attackers was more a case of good conditioning and probably eating well. He reached immediately for Wilhelmina, but another Luger smashed it from his hand and a short, hardwood baton, half the length and half the weight of a riot stick, hit him across the right bicep, a stinging blow from an expert toss.

Positioning himself to use his feet, Carter got off one well-placed kick to the shoulder of one of the five. Working on instinct, he chopped at another attacker with his still numb right. His target went down, but Carter felt the impact roar through his arm. Turning to take a flying kick from a third attacker, he caught a leg in both hands, yanked upward, and converted the kicker's momentum into a continued upward thrust. The kicker came down hard and vulnerable on his tail bone, letting out a yowl of pain, his eyes filled with the fury of frustration.

Now Carter fended off a looping right from a fourth attacker, but the one who'd thrown the baton had come up into

49

position and blind-sided him, driving him down, where a 9mm Luger was thrust in his face.

"Hold, Killmaster!" a voice said in a now familiar accent. Carter smiled and extended his hands. As he did, he saw one of the attackers holding a Luger on Margo Huerta. Carter could not tell if she were being held for cosmetic purposes or not. The attacker who held the gun on her nudged her toward a row of parked cars. "It would be amusing to turn the tables on this one and hold an auction for her," he said. "I wonder how many of her liberal friends would bid anything."

"Depends on what they'd be bidding for," another said, and they all laughed.

"Up on your feet, Killmaster," the tallest of the group said, and began nudging Carter toward a four-wheel-drive vehicle. Margo was loaded into a Blazer where a driver already waited, the engine at idle. They pulled out into the late--afternoon traffic first.

Carter was nudged into a Toyota Landcruiser, a vehicle that had seen some extensive use but was obviously in a good state of repair. It accelerated smoothly, was tuned quietly, and did not emit huge billows of fumes.

As they angled away from Bucareli toward Reforma, Carter saw that no attempt was made to keep the Blazer in sight. Perhaps they were even being taken to separate destinations. Only when they turned onto Avenida Insurgentes Sur and Carter caught a fleeting glimpse of the Blazer did he realize that both vehicles were going to the same place.

"I don't suppose you're giving any hints about where we're going," Carter said.

His captors did not respond.

"I suspect," Carter said, trying to get a rise out of them, "that if we're away long enough for dinner, we're bound to see some lamb flavored with cumin."

One of them started to speak, but his seatmate nudged him to silence.

Carter asked for a cigarette, giving his Arabic a particularly Palestinian spin. Without thinking, the one who had started to answer him moments before reached into his shirt pocket and brought out a crumpled blue pack of Gitanes. Carter laughed aloud, and once again the sterner of Carter's captors scowled.

"You have all the small victories you want, Killmaster," he said. "We have you. The big victory is ours."

The Toyota lost contact with the Blazer until the merge point where Highway 57 turned into the deluxe toll road, 57D, moving north from Mexico City. The Blazer passed the Toyota and remained about six car lengths in front.

The terrain gradually grew more mountainous and rugged, but the highway was splendid, a series of well-crafted grades, turnouts, and gently elevating straightaways. The only thing that spoke of any difficulties were the road signs, often appearing to give conflicting information.

Highway 57D entered the State of Mexico, left it, and entered it again for a time. The city limits of the capital, also called the Federal District, were alternately straight ahead, to the left, and directly behind them. Carter had no clue as to where they were going. The major destinations within reasonable driving time were the village of San Juan del Rio and, about an hour's fast drive beyond that, the increasingly trendy arts and retirement center of San Miguel de Allende. Even though the drive was smooth, the surgical work on Carter's shoulder began to throb, and the Killmaster decided the best thing to do was settle into a light doze in preparation for what lay ahead.

Carter felt himself move forward into full alert just at the exit to San Juan del Rio, where the Blazer took a turnoff after failing to heed honked warnings from the Toyota. The driver of the Toyota and the surliest of Carter's captors were visibly and verbally irritated with the Blazer, and attempts at signaling with hands, handkerchiefs, and neck scarves began.

After continued honking and waving of scarves, the Blazer stopped and the captors pulled out a road map and began consulting it.

"I see you have trouble with the Mexican road system," Carter said.

The captor sitting next to him cuffed him. "Laugh all you wish, Mr. Professional. We hold you prisoner. We do not intimidate through your cheap humor."

"Ah, but it isn't my humor," the Killmaster said, "it happens to be *your* humor. At least, it's humor at your expense. It is my professional attitude and it helps keep me alive. One thing you might remember. Until I'm dead, I'm a professional. If I go, I'll take a lot of you with me."

There was no rancor in Carter's voice or eyes. He was so matter-of-fact that his message found his mark. His captor offered him a cigarette.

Just north of the city the Toyota drew abreast of the Blazer and the two cars pulled over to the side of a narrow, two-lane road, a maneuver that proved to be imprudent when a large pickup, its bed loaded with chicken cages, careened around a dirt road, began honking at the two parked vehicles, and slammed on its brakes, but not before delivering a sharp crease to the left rear of the Blazer, miraculously avoiding smashing its taillights. A short, feisty man with a Pancho Villa mustache and a faded pair of mechanic's overalls bounded out of the cab, complaining vigorously, actually pounding the back of the Blazer.

Carter was handcuffed to the metal tubing under his seat as all but the driver of the Toyota got out to deal with the driver of the pickup. A number of children from a nearby yard appeared, watching with open-mouthed wonder. Carter was not amused to note that Margo Huerta was nowhere to be seen in the Blazer.

The driver of the Toyota had a 9mm Luger trained on Carter.

"You'd better not let the *federales* see you waving that," Carter said conversationally. "They don't take kindly to guns being waved in their country unless they're doing the waving. And you can be sure they'll be along if someone doesn't deal properly with the driver of that pickup. They or the Green Angels. You can be sure of it."

The driver coaxed a cigarette out of a package and thumbed a wooden match. "You'd better not try anything, Carter."

"You're doing well enough without me," the Killmaster said, noting with unconcealed amusement that another vehicle, a white-and-green-striped repair truck with wide-track heavy-treaded wheels pulled up to join the congregation.

"Speak of the devil," Carter said. "I do believe the Green Angels have come to someone's rescue."

Carter noted that his captors were completely intimidated by the appearance of the Green Angel truck and by the two men riding in it, one of whom, a tall, robust man with an L.A. Dodgers baseball cap, emerged and advanced on the group.

The Green Angels are the Mexican equivalent of an auto club, an emergency road repair service, but even more, they are occasional arbitrators in disputes between motorists and local garages, rescuers of tourists who were stranded or thought they were.

Large quantities of Mexican money appeared to be changing hands as the Green Angels and Carter's captors gesticulated and the owner of the pickup truck began yowling in a plaintive voice.

The Green Angel in the baseball cap approached the truckdriver with the money he'd extracted from the captors.

The truck driver looked at the money, turned from it with disdain, strode purposefully over to the Toyota, and kicked the side panel.

"Be honest, now," Carter told his driver. "Do your companions understand Spanish very well? You appear to be in a problem that can only worsen."

"Two of them speak it well enough."

"Ask him what he considers appropriate damages—and pay him," Carter said. "If the police come and you are found not to have Mexican liability insurance, you will be in a situation far worse than Señorita Huerta and I are in."

Still holding the Luger at the level of Carter's navel, the driver of the Toyota called out to his companions in a guttural, colloquial Arabic.

At length, two of them approached and Carter heard the driver working to convince his colleagues to offer more money and get out of this mess.

When an acceptable amount was finally offered, the driver of the pickup truck got back inside the cab of his vehicle, revved his engine a few times and drove off. The Green Angels followed, and the procession began again, this time with the Toyota taking the lead.

They continued north, following signs indicating San Miguel de Allende, but after a few more miles in that direction, the area surrounding the roadbed began to give way to occasional fences, a few gutted shells of adobe sheds, and the beginnings of abundant pastureland where small, leathery-looking cows grazed.

At an unmarked road, the Toyota turned right, which Carter reckoned was close to due north. With the Blazer behind, they remained on a narrow, well-graded but unpaved road, running toward the nearby range of mountains.

The terrain began to increase in rockiness and now, on either side of them, the fields of short, clumpy grass were still suitable for grazing—indeed, an occasional cow pushed her nose into the choicer morsels and munched—but the boulders increased in size and number. What had started as a gentle afternoon breeze began to gain strength, pushing waves and ripples across the longer grass and filling the air with seeds, pollen, and chaff. The driver of the Toyota sneezed and cursed his allergy.

After another several miles of driving in low gear, they came to a large watering hole, and the road curved away from it, moving now toward a distant clump of the distinctive agave cactus and trees that Carter supposed had been planted years back as a windbreak.

As they approached the trees, a scraggly stand of cottonwood, juniper, and gums, the terrain took an even more pronounced upward thrust. Dust devils danced as the wind began to intensify. Looking back, Carter could see how they had gradually climbed to the point where the mountains were close at hand.

Their destination became immediately clear as they rounded another bend. A large, low-slung building, probably some kind of line camp, was positioned to catch the afternoon shade cast by the trees. It was large enough to have a number of rooms. A chimney and vents suggested the interior had ample heating and cooking facilities. This far out in the country, there were no traces of power lines, but any of the three or four outbuildings could house a generator. Essentially made from adobe brick, the building had shuttered windows and a thatched willow rod roof. A small fresh stream ran nearby, and a large well, with masonry made from the nearby rocks, attested to the strategic position.

Evidence of corrals and pens were plentiful, but at the moment, neither horse nor cow seemed much in evidence. On the other hand, two other four-wheel-drive vehicles were parked in front of the building, not far from the main door.

Carter was freed from his handcuffs and nudged out into

the early evening. The sound of the nearby stream reminded him how thirsty he was. He noted with some interest that Margo had been in the Blazer all along and reasoned that she'd been hidden under some lap robes after the run-in with the pickup truck had taken place. Perhaps he'd been wrong to suspect her of complicity in this, but with the same kind of instinct that he'd used to suspect there had been something not entirely right about Rachel Porat, he decided he needed to find out more about Margo Huerta before he could trust her. His life might depend on it.

Margo was pushed, cramped from the long ride, into the lengthening shadows of the afternoon. The wind tossed her hair and caused her to blink her eyes. She began a steady stream of invective as she was nudged toward the front porch of the house, telling her captors they'd picked the wrong one to mess with, and trying to incite them to some kind of anger.

Those among her captors who could understand her chose to ignore her words. Even those who had limited Spanish could probably have divined her intent, but they remained impassive, pushing her toward the building.

One of the captors reached the door with a few bounding steps, opened it, and nudged Margo inside. Carter was brought along directly behind.

The door opened into a rather large, comfortable room with a stone fireplace, a well-designed cooking area, and a long plank table as well as several sturdy chairs made out of willow rods over which rawhide had been stretched and soaked to the point of tautness.

Two other men awaited them, wearing nondescript khakis and denim work shirts. A pot of coffee boiled over a charcoal fire. Yet another man stood, using a large, handcarved wooden spoon to stir a large copper pan from which a piquant stew gave off the pungent aroma of cumin and cilantro. A large stack of plastic bowls were nested nearby.

"What now?" Margo said.

"Looks like we're going to get some lamb after all," Carter replied, allowing himself to be guided to a seat.

The door to an adjoining room burst open and a man with a sharp, angular face, bushy brows, a cleft chin, and pale blue eyes appeared.

"Sorry to have missed you in Paris, Carter."

"Who is this guy?" Margo asked.

"Tell her, Carter," the man with the cleft chin said. "I'm certain you know."

"Margo, meet Abdul Samadhi. I suspect that's his real name. He probably has a much more imaginative street name."

"It's going to be a great pleasure questioning you both," the PLO man said.

# SEVEN

Carter and Margo were separated, Carter being moved into a side room with small high windows and several layers of whitewash covering the adobe surface. In addition to a plank table and a few primitive chairs, there was a cot, a table covered with old magazines, and a wooden crate serving as a base for a portable shortwave radio.

Abdul Samadhi, working on a two-day growth of beard, motioned Carter to a seat at the plank table, produced cigarettes, and leveled his strange blue eyes at Carter. "What were you doing in Paris?"

"Vacationing."

"Yes, and your experiences there were so taxing that you had to come to Mexico to get away from everything," Samadhi said, standing and beginning to pace about the room, tapping a willow switch against his palm. "What do you know of Lex Talionis, Killmaster?"

"The law of the lion," Carter said. "A concept in early jurisprudence that finds a perfect expression in the Old Testament. Basically, it's the concept of an eye for an eye, a tooth for a tooth."

Samadhi swiped at the tabletop with the willow switch. "Don't play games with me."

Carter spread his palms. "Obviously, you don't know what it is yet."

"Perhaps I am checking to see if you are innocent enough to be allowed to remain free." Samadhi fingered the cleft in his chin.

"Perhaps you're trying to cash in on what you think is a big thing, Samadhi, the biggest thing you've ever had thrown your way. I know some of you PLO fellows are reasonable in your dedication and conviction. But even among the best of a group of idealists, the scent of a big score becomes more than the ideals can stand."

"There are ways to make you talk," Samadhi said.

"Bribes?" Carter suggested, smiling.

"If I thought that would be effective."

"Torture?" Carter continued.

"As a last resort. But first we eat." The PLO operative called sharply in slangy Arabic. Moments later, the door opened and the man Carter had seen stirring the lamb stew entered carrying a tray with two steaming bowls, a pile of fresh-baked pita bread, a bowl of diced green chiles, and a single large pot of beans with sliced onions.

Samadhi urged Carter to chose his own serving to avoid any suspicion. When Carter slid a bowl in front of him, Samadhi began working the remaining bowl and the beans, eating quickly for a few moments, once again attempting to show Carter that none of the portions was tainted with any chemical or drug.

"You have to understand something about us, Carter. Our frustrations increase exponentially as each generation of youngsters comes to us, wanting to win the honorable way, through justice. But as you can see, justice is at best a concept for the classroom—and at that the classrooms of the highly privileged."

"You often fight among yourselves," Carter reminded him.

Abdul Samadhi nodded thoughtfully. "It is true. I try to explain to some of our younger ones. Just as violence and terrorism are options, so are negotiation and conciliation. But it is so easy to be violent when you are desperate, Carter. And what they cannot see is that they are walking on a two-way street. They use violence and terrorism as weapons, but they are blinded to the fact that it is ever so easy to use violence and terrorism against them. Then no one has gained and both sides have dug their heels in a bit deeper."

"I don't think you brought us here to discuss the Golan Heights," Carter said, beginning to realize how hungry he was. He started to eat the savory lamb, thinking how Samadhi was probably once a man of great honor and integrity in his home area. If he'd been born in any of a dozen other countries or locales, even those poorer than where he actually was born, Samadhi would have been another kind of leader—a man respected and followed. A teacher instead of a terrorist.

"You say we are opportunists and fight among ourselves," the PLO operative observed. "It is all true. I believe there have been studies in your country, studies that significantly use laboratory rats or street people because they are equally desperate. The studies show that the oppressed, the desperate, the needy will frequently engage one another in violence when the medium of their freedom or salvation is within their grasp."

"I've conducted some studies of my own," Carter said. "Remember, I was present when your lot took out Nino Sichi."

Samadhi's light blue eyes flashed with amusement. "Such righteous indignation and moral posturing, Carter. My studies show that your country tried, as you put it, to take out Fidel Castro. My studies show your country successfully took out President Allende of Chile."

The PLO operative took several mouthfuls of stew, chewing reflectively. "If we had time, Carter, I would enjoy playing chess with you and discussing politics. The chess would probably be the purer of the pursuits because the moment we started in on politics, you'd point to so-called Marxist leanings in my arguments and then you would completely tune me out as the implacable foe of Western democracy." He daubed at his chin with a napkin, consulted his watch, and smiled at a thought that came to him.

"I can tell you that the people who gave you the essence of your precious Westernized democracy were scoundrels and pragmatists, demonstrably addicted to violence." He set his eating utensils down with a look of finality, smiled again, his light blue eyes flashing, and leaned across the table. "Yes, we did indeed remove that little worm, Sichi. You probably know better than I that he had a cynical eye and a hand in every pocket. He tried to betray us over a large matter. Many of us in the PLO have come to conclude that we must strengthen our cause by allying ourselves with the power. We must take the kind of overview our oppressors are unwilling to take. Even if, as the saying goes, politics makes for strange bedfellows, we must learn to reassess who our enemies are and with whom it is more provident for us to align ourselves."

His face seemed to lose the easygoing affability of the past moments and freeze into an intensity that had violence and determination. "It is time to be forthcoming, Carter. Tell me what you know about Lex Talionis."

Carter tried to push away a wave of heaviness that came, no doubt, from the amount of stew he'd eaten. But he felt a sudden surge of adrenaline when he heard a scream from the next room.

"Yes, right on time," Abdul Samadhi said. "You will hear that sound quite often unless you begin to give me information."

Carter waved his hand impatiently. "Forget it. That gambit won't work. Suppose she's with you. I sit here and spill all the beans while she files her nails, reads a magazine, and lets out a blood-curdling yell now and then. Sorry to disappoint you."

Samadhi exploded with impatience. He moved at Carter, thinking to lead him to the door, but Carter's instincts were too fast for thought. He danced behind Samadhi, his left hand catching him under the elbow, his right applying fulcrum force and suddenly the PLO man was wrenched painfully to the floor. Samadhi sat cradling his injured wrist, swearing bitterly.

"You terrorists are all pretty good at the first strike," Carter growled, "but if someone strikes back and one of you gets hurt, it's suddenly not fair."

For a moment Carter thought Samadhi had lost control—a bad thing for any fighter to do. He saw the man trying to calm himself. Before Samadhi was completely ready, he spoke.

"Fair? You talk to me of fair?" A scowl of determination twisted his face. He rose, dusted himself off, then spoke to Carter with ironic politeness. "Please, sir, come with me. I'll show you what's fair." He moved to the door, indicating for Carter to follow. "Fair, my dear sir, is a concept that applies to the man who has the most guns."

Samadhi showed Carter a chilling sight. He opened the door and shoved Carter into the next room.

Margo Huerta was spread-eagled on a cot, wrists and ankles firmly tied to the four sides. One of the PLO had a twelve-volt battery and a device that appeared to Carter to use the ignition coil of an automobile. A ground wire from the battery and a lead from the coil were being applied to the skin between the toes of Margo's right foot. A faint crackling sound issued forth and Carter caught the scent of burning flesh. Margo strained against her bonds and let out another yell of the sort Carter had heard in the other room.

"Do you still think she's with us, Carter?"

Samadhi pushed Carter back into the next room, kicked the door shut, and pounded on the table. As if in response, another cry came from Margo Huerta. "For God's sake, Carter!" she screamed. "Tell them what they want to know!"

Carter sank to a chair, aware that for the past few moments his head was growing heavier. "Still don't believe you, Samadhi," he said. "Not convinced that contraption of yours is anything more than a bunch of wires."

Margo screamed again and Carter found himself having to fight to keep his eyes open.

"How did you do it?" he asked.

"The pita bread." Samadhi stood over him now. "You were concerned with the stew. It was easy to serve you pita bread with some additional ingredients. Listen to me, Carter. That is all real. If you were not so drowsy now, I'd show you firsthand. But your mind knows the truth. The Huerta woman is in real pain and you are the instrument. All you have to do is tell me what I want to know."

Carter felt the heaviness tumbling down upon him like a collapsing house of cards.

"What is Lex Talionis, Carter?"

The Killmaster had had several sessions with his psychologist friend, Ira Wein, in learning techniques to avoid such types of questioning. Wein had instructed him to focus his mind on some poem from his student days, something as juvenile as possible.

Chances were good that even if he'd been drugged with scopolamine or other so-called truth drugs, he'd repeat the poem over and over again, causing his questioners to think he'd reverted to a time in his youth from which they could not budge him.

"They ask you questions to get your mind on the subject of interest to them," Wein had told him. "The trick is for you to get your mind on anything else but where they want it, understand?"

"Tell me about Lex Talionis, Carter."

Carter got off a few stanzas of "Twinkle, Twinkle Little Star" before Samadhi began shaking and slapping him. In the background, he was again aware of Margo screaming.

He mustn't think of that screaming.

Focus on something else.

Focus on that flapping sound in the distance, whatever it was. The flapping noise that seemed to remind Carter of someone beating a rug with rapid, steady strokes. That increasing sound that suddenly seemed to make Abdul Samadhi angry enough that he began swearing and pushing Carter around.

"Lex Talionis, Carter. Tell me what you know."

"Organization to get revenge," Carter responded against his will.

Then the kindly image of Ira Wein came to him and he began to rock with laughter, although he didn't know why.

He saw the entrance to a large black cave and in his mind's eye, he entered it.

Everything was dark for a time, but someone was setting off fireworks and there was a good deal of activity with people shouting, and the stew was burning in the next room.

After a time, Carter realized he wasn't smelling burning stew at all but rather the distinctive smell of weapons being discharged. There was at least one muffled report nearby, and in his sleep-clouded mind, Carter tried to rouse himself to action.

He sank to the floor, tried to push himself to a sitting position, and collapsed again.

He was working on pure instinct and coordination now. He fought his way to a sitting position and tried to focus his watery eyes.

He was aware of a rather large presence carrying him to a cot and setting him on top of it.

Then the activities began to recede again and Carter no longer had the ability to fight it.

# EIGHT

Nick Carter's head felt as though it had been stuffed with the small plastic chips used to insulate shipping cartons. He tentatively flexed his hands, finding them stiff and numb. A tortured sound appeared to come from outside, but Carter quickly realized it had been the sound of his own groan. His head was tender to the touch and his mouth seemed dry and thick.

"Here, try this, Carter," a sympathetic voice said, handing him a clay drinking cup. "Go ahead, it's rather sweet well water."

Carter drank gratefully, then turned to regard his companion. "Who . . . ?" he began, but stopped when it came out sounding like a barking seal.

"Zachary. Sam Zachary. CIA. Sorry we couldn't get here any sooner. Some horrendous winds developed and they naturally slowed us down. But I don't think any serious harm's been done."

Carter heard a burst of automatic fire from the near distance.

"We've got your friends hemmed in up toward the draw."

"We?"

"Two associates of mine and a lad who's interested in meeting you. Cuban, but he spends a good deal of time with us."

"The woman?" Carter asked.

"She had a bad scare, but she's all right." Zachary poured more water for Carter, then poured two cups of coffee from a stainless steel Thermos on the table. "I might be able to

63

scrounge up some sugar, but if you like your coffee with milk, you're out of luck."

"I'll take it any way I can get it," Carter said, accepting the hot, steaming mug from Zachary and guiding it to his lips with both hands. The robust flavor immediately cheered him. "This is Jamaican blue mountain."

Zachary nodded. "Coffee is such a vile concoction that you might as well drink the best if you drink it at all."

Carter sipped appreciatively, watching the CIA man, an agreeable sort, slightly taller than himself. Hand-tailored blazer, sturdy twill chinos, and a crisply laundered cotton shirt in muted stripes. "I know you from somewhere."

"I should think so," Zachary said. "I saw you briefly about two years ago at a David Hawk meeting to discuss ethics in intelligence gathering, but more recently"—Zachary reached into his pocket, removed a convincing false mustache, and plastered it on his upper lip—"the Green Angels, at your service."

"The driver of the chicken truck?"

"Ah, yes. Chepe Muñoz. Good man. Wanted to meet you and—well, you know the drill in this business. Now, as the saying goes, you owe him one."

By now Carter was taking larger sips of Zachary's excellent coffee and the fogginess in his head was beginning to recede. "It makes sense now. All that business with the kicking and thumping was a blind to let you put beepers on both vehicles. Then you tracked us with choppers."

"You have to admit, Carter, it worked. It would have been even sooner if not for that damned wind. I keep telling them to buy us the Hueys. A nice, substantial chopper. So what do they do? They have to get these little pipsqueak AF-sixes." Zachary shook his head. "Everyone's so damned cost-conscious since Cap Weinberger got caught with those expensive ashtrays and toilet seats."

Carter lowered his voice. "I'm not sure we can trust Margo Huerta."

Two exchanges of automatic weapons fire, one distant, the other considerably closer, punctuated his comment.

"Why not? Why wouldn't you trust her?"

"I think she's a radical groupie. But that's a possible cover for some other things."

Zachary smiled. "I know for a fact she propositioned Chepe Muñoz, and I've seen her at some conspicuously liberal parties, but we don't have anything of value in our field reports to suggest anything fishy."

"Just a hunch, so far." Carter finished his coffee, feeling measurably better. He got tentatively to his feet, did a few slow torso stretches, and allowed Zachary to pour more coffee.

"I almost feel I can cope again," Carter said.

Zachary smiled. "Excellent. We'd better give the others a hand. We can talk later."

The CIA operative led Carter outside, where two AF-6 choppers were moored. Zachary tossed Carter an FN-FAL, which Carter checked quickly and with respect. It was an excellent weapon. He fired a burst, liked the placement.

"We got one of the PLOs when we came in," Zachary said, "but there are four left and we'd very much like to get our hands on the leader."

"Abdul Samadhi."

Zachary beamed. "You're sure?"

Carter nodded.

"We thought it might be him, but we lost him between Paris and here. Yes, we'd definitely like to have a few words with him."

As they started up the draw, Carter could see two of Zachary's colleagues, nicely positioned behind clumps of rock. "Muñoz is further up and to your left."

One of Carter's captors appeared suddenly and sprayed a blast, drawing return fire. Carter watched another Palestinian scrabble up a segment of rock, take a hard leap, then disappear. Carter thought he saw a grenade launcher. They would have to be careful about letting the PLO get close to the choppers.

Zachary and Carter quickly agreed on assignments and moved off into position. As he broke into a running crouch, Carter noticed Margo Huerta, protected by a small boulder, smoking a cigarette, hugging her knees to her chest. She waved a vulgar gesture to Carter. "You still think I set this up, you pig."

Carter's response was blunted by a stitching of shots directed at Sam Zachary, who zigzagged into his assigned position. Now a spray of shots forced the Killmaster down, but he took the chance after waiting a few moments and broke for the protective cover of a large tree stump.

A thumping sound warned Carter that the grenade launcher had been fired.

The blast from the explosion felt like hands being clapped over both ears. A spray of debris erupted between Carter and Zachary. Up ahead, the bearlike man in camouflage trousers and a blue sweat shirt took a risk, but made it pay off. He broke from cover and angled toward the position of the grenade launcher, opened another stitching of fire across the face of the rocks, scrambled up an outcropping, paused, took deliberate aim, and squeezed a short burst. The unmistakable sound of a hit came. A man yowled, staggered forward, and fell.

Wanting to contribute more than backup to his rescuers, Carter took off at a crouch, slamming a new ammo clip into place and doing a side roll on his good shoulder when one of the PLO opened up on him, and got to another portion of the outcropping. He took a spring up toward a new plateau and, as he'd suspected, bought himself a clear shot.

His burst caught the man who'd been driving the Toyota earlier. Chepe Muñoz, the bearlike man in the camouflage trousers, gave Carter a high sign of appreciation and motioned him forward. Both men were angling toward a gully that alternately rose and fell.

After about five minutes of running and probing, Muñoz let out a loud curse in Spanish and started back at a run toward the choppers, calling after one of Zachary's assistants.

After a hurried conference, Muñoz and Zachary's assistant fired up one of the choppers, gained altitude quickly, and moved off along the fault line of the ravine.

"Samadhi probably grew up in terrain just like this," Zachary said. "We account for all the others now but him, and he's the one we want, dammit."

Zachary drew some water from the well, took it inside the building, and put it on to boil. From his war chest he brought forth a battery-powered coffee grinder and enough of the Jamaican beans for another Thermos full of the pungent brew.

"I don't think we've seen anything like the last of him," Carter said. "I get my best results when I back off for a while.

Samadhi's had his early rounds, but we'll get him. Meanwhile, why don't you brief me on your aims in all this."

The CIA man nodded at Carter's wisdom. When the coffee was brewed, he brought Carter up to date. "I was brought in on this play of yours because we've apparently been burned for a good deal of cash lately." Responding to Carter's raised eyebrows, Zachary continued. "Someone's nicked us for over a million and it's been heading down this way and father south."

"El Salvador? Nicaragua?"

The affable CIA man shook his shaggy head. "Not quite that far south, and not anything so obvious. Of all places, Belize. This makes it really sensitive because we—that is, the United States—are not as favored as we once were in Guatemala, and guess who has their cap set on having Belize returned to them."

Carter sipped his coffee, nodding.

"It is also widely believed, by no less than your own David Hawk, that we—that is, the CIA—are responsible for the precipitous removal of a certain cadaver from Covington, Kentucky. Mr. Hawk was all over my supervisor on that."

"You have to admit," Carter said, "there's reason to suspect your motives."

"As a consequence of that and some healthy skepticism from your leader, I was sent to Covington to question the local sheriff and the manager of the resort where the Grinning Gaucho's heart took its last pump. They still believe it was the Justice Department who questioned them."

"Have your people checked with NSC?" Carter asked.

Zachary smiled. "That's a rather touchy suggestion, and it convinces me you still have your doubts about us." Before Zachary could explain any further, the sound of the returning chopper began to intrude.

They went outside to watch the small craft dropping to a landing some fifty yards from the house. The side door sprang open and Chepe Muñoz jumped out, a look of disgust on his face.

"Son of a bitch got away," he said. "He is one smart cookie." Springing toward Zachary and Carter, the burly Cuban held out his hand.

"I've looked forward to this, Carter." The Cuban's grip

was firm and powerful, his eyes taking in the terrain with steady sweeps. A man used to living in some dangerous climates, politically and physically, Carter thought. "My *compadre* here tells me you like to talk about stuff like the civil society and how those concepts go all the way back to the seventeenth century and in the works of dudes like Hobbes and Lock."

Carter agreed. "It's always important to keep up on history of important movements, and the civil society is important."

"But you don't think people are subordinate to philosophies, do you?" the Cuban pressed.

"I think," Nick Carter said, "that philosophies should help people lead the lives of highest moral quality, otherwise they're useless."

Chepe Muñoz nodded approvingly at Zachary, then gave Carter a big, warm embrace. "We're going to work well together, *hombre*."

"This is starting to remind me of that old Marx Brothers movie with all the people being jammed into the one small stateroom of a luxury cruiser," Carter said.

"Hey, man, ain't it the truth," Muñoz agreed. "Lot of people popping out of the woodwork in this caper. I sure didn't expect to see my buddy Zachary in on this one, and I sure didn't expect you. What did they sting your people for?"

Carter merely smiled.

"Then you're the only ones," Muñoz said. "They got Zachary's people good. They got my people. They got the Red Brigade. I hear, round about through Havana, that they even got the Chinese."

"Not to forget the South African diamond cartel," Carter said, deciding to throw in a bit of intrigue and perhaps get Zachary or Muñoz to open up further. Also, it would be an excellent way of checking his suspicions about Margo Huerta.

Muñoz grabbed Carter's arm. "Hey, are you serious? The diamond cartel?" He shook his head in disbelief. "Nobody stings those guys."

Carter studied Muñoz's reaction and decided to trust the stocky Cuban. He was also beginning to think he might have been hasty in his judgment of Margo. She'd known who Piet Bezeidenhout was and both Muñoz and Zachary had been surprised to learn of the South African connection. Even though she'd said she'd take Carter to meet Muñoz, she hadn't shared this information with the Cuban.

Inside the house, as Zachary began his ritual of making more coffee, Carter thought it best to strike while the sense of camaraderie among them was warm. "All we need to do now is find out who they are and what they want. I have a theory, but it's all circumstantial."

"That's as good if not better than anything we have," Zachary said, dealing out the coffee.

While Carter spoke, Zachary's assistant, at Zachary's gestured orders, went into the war chest and came out with several freeze-dried packets and a few canned and bottled items, humming to himself as he looked about the crude kitchen where he'd be working on their next meal.

"Let's assume that there is an individual at the top of the organizational chart of Lex Talionis, a man or woman with the financial background and audacity of an Ivan Boesky. Perhaps this person has already brought a great deal of money into the picture, thinking of it as venture capital." Carter could see that he already had their attention. "Very well, now instead of organizing along strictly political lines like, say, PLO against the Mossad, KGB against the CIA, or even along divisions within a country like the infighting between the FBI, the CIA, the State Department, the Justice Department, and the NSC every time we elect a new president—instead of that, we see the concept of a multinational organization based on the lines of strict profitability."

"I'm with you in principle," Zachary said. "But what's the inducement? Why, suddenly, would dogs and cats begin to cooperate?

"Pure capitalism and a bit of Japanese-style management concepts. All the top-level people who come in have to have two kinds of credentials," Carter continued. "They have to have a street reputation, as it were—connections with some military or political power—and something else to throw in the pot."

"Money!" Muñoz said, getting the picture.

"Arms!" Zachary said.

"Industrial and commercial diamonds," Carter added, reminding them about the diamonds Prentiss had tried to pass along and also adding his account about the small bag of diamonds at the Sichi murder.

Zachary's assistant served a large bowl of pasta with a piquant sauce and called Margo Huerta to join them.

"So you're suggesting an operation that runs like a franchise, one of these multilevel marketing organizations?" Zachary ventured.

"Right," Carter said. "And the incentive is profit."

"Which means," Zachary said as Margo entered the room, "that they're going to start wanting a return on their money quite soon."

Muñoz plunked a hairy fist on the table. "They sent me for a crash course at the London School of Economics," he told them, "and that confirmed most of my suspicions about what *pendejos*, what pubic hairs those large multinational organizations are, but this"—he looked at Carter—"this beats all. I hope you're wrong, *amigo*."

Carter started in on his pasta. "That's why I need your help."

Zachary stood to make room for Margo, but she seemed preoccupied, looking about the room for a moment while the men fell to their meal. As they ate, the conversation fell off, staying with compliments for the man who had prepared it from the seemingly inexhaustible war chest Zachary carried with him.

"I'm afraid this is it," Zachary said. "If we stay here any longer, it's either that lamb or nothing."

"What is there to keep us?" Muñoz asked.

"We should do a thorough check on those corpses and then we should bury them," Carter advised. He was aware of the others nodding agreement. "Then we need a working plan— which I've just been formulating. I think it's time to get back to Mexico City, check in with my source, and try to pick up Piet Bezeidenhout's trail. If this is the parting of the ways for us right now, I think we'll be in touch on this very case not too far down the line."

As they sat waiting for him to give more details, Carter suddenly felt a searing, jagged sensation at his neck, literally causing his right hand to twitch and drop the crude fork it held.

"There, Mr. Nick Carter," Margo Huerta said.

Turning, Carter saw her holding the electrodes from the battery and coil that had been used to torture her.

Fiercely, Margo touched the leads together, producing a series of sparks and a burning smell. "There," she said. "I suppose you'll tell your friends here that this is still some phony device that can't possibly work."

She touched the electrodes once again to Carter's arm. He jerked reflexively away from them. "I could have cooked your lousy dinner with this contraption, Carter."

Carter nodded, stood, extended his hand. "I was wrong to think the way I did."

"Goddamn right," Margo said, setting the contraption down with a bang, then suddenly beginning to shake with emotion.

"We're all uptight and frustrated right now," Zachary said. "Let's get those bodies buried and get the hell out of here."

An hour later, the dead PLO guerrillas buried, Chepe Muñoz and Margo Huerta climbed into the first helicopter while Carter and Zachary checked the buildings one more time for leads to Abdul Samadhi's base in Mexico. They found nothing except a stack of leaflets for a poetry reading by James Rogan of the U.S.A., the Pennsylvania Powerhouse, next day in Mexico City, and a brochure describing Rogan's arts center and festival of performing arts in Belize.

Carter looked at Zachary. "You see Samadhi and his gang going to poetry readings?"

"About as much as I see myself," Zachary snorted.

"I think it's worth the effort to check out this Rogan character. We—"

It was as far as the Killmaster got.

Heavy firing suddenly exploded outside. The two agents grabbed their weapons and ran to the windows. A helicopter engine roared into high. The chopper carrying Chepe Muñoz and Margo Huerta rose into the air, and swung away at a sharp angle almost hitting the trees as bullets ripped through the rotors. Carter and Zachary held their breaths as the chopper dipped, almost hit a low ridge, then picked up speed and vanished, climbing over the surrounding mountain peaks.

"They made it," Zachary exulted.

"But I don't think we're going to," Carter said grimly.

Outside, at least a company of *federales* emerged from the

brush and surrounded the buildings. A spit-and-polish lieutenant held up a bullhorn:

"You are completely surrounded. There is no escape. I give you the option to come out with your hands up."

The Killmaster shrugged.

"Sometimes you have to know when to fold your hand." He dropped his weapon and stepped out of the building with his hands up.

# NINE

The trip back to Mexico City in the back of the troop carrier under the watchful eyes of four young *federales* was uneventful. In the small neat office they were hustled into, Carter guessed things were going to be a lot more exciting.

In the office the Killmaster and Zachary faced a heavily mustached man with graying sideburns, bright red suspenders, and a military identity tag with the name CAPITAN MOISES ALVARADO H. Carter decided to try the usual innocent, outraged approach.

"All right Captain Alvarado, let's get on with it. Why were we brought here, manhandled, and placed under arrest? Those bandits were throwing heavy weapons at us. Our rights—"

"Just shut up, Señor Carter, eh? Am I such a fool to you? We find you and your friends heavily armed and engaged in a lethal exchange of fire with some other equally armed foreigners and you have the nerve to ask why *we* brought *you* here? As you say in your country, 'Gimme a break!'" The captain glared almost in amazement at both Carter and Zachary. "And that, as we say in this country, is only the tail of the iguana. What you are really here for, in addition to a possible charge of armed insurrection, is because I have this strange awareness and suspicion of other activities in which you may be involved." There was not a trace of humor in Alvarado's obsidian eyes. "Unless I miss my guess, señores, you two are going to stonewall and be cute and as a result, something's going to happen to you that I assure you is rare in the history of our country." He waited a moment for emphasis, then leaned closer. "You're both going to get your asses booted out of Mexico, and none of your influence or string-pulling is going to make any difference."

Captain Alvarado began to toy with a pencil. "Maybe I'm wrong. Maybe you're going to tell me what the hell's going on, why you both come into my country with a virtual arsenal and begin poking around on a venture without having the common courtesy to check in with our intelligence people in the first place. That's not only an arrogant thing to do, it's a dumb thing to do."

The Mexican intelligence officer impressed Carter as being an honest man, trying to do a straightforward job. "Let's start with you, Mr. Zachary. It is Mister, isn't it? No military titles or diplomatic stuff?"

"Actually," Zachary said, "it's Doctor. I never got very far in the military, but I did pick up a Ph.D. as I suspect you already know."

"Very good," Alvarado said. "From small truths come great confidences. What was your mission regarding Abdul Samadhi?"

Zachary shook his head. "This is the part you're going to have trouble with, Captain Alvarado. I had no mission as such with Samadhi. I was trailing him to see where he went and with whom he'd make contact."

"Why were you doing this?"

Zachary spread his palms. "It gets even worse from here on. I have no idea why I was trailing him. I can speculate, but that's as far as it goes."

"What about you, Señor Carter? What was your interest in the PLO?"

"I was hoping to learn why he's here myself."

Alvarado nodded without comment. "When did you first learn they were in Mexico?"

"Very early this morning," Carter said.

"Later this afternoon," Zachary said.

"I am fortunate that my position here is professional, not political," Captain Alvarado sighed. "I have experience in the gathering of intelligence reports, the following of leads, the piecing together of seemingly unrelated bits of information."

Carter did not like the way this was beginning to sound.

Alvarado was now clearly struggling to keep his voice level. "You are both here before me as fellow professionals.

You are both telling me you are interested in a man you are both following without knowing why."

Carter decided there was no way out of enraging the captain, but he hoped to give just enough information to secure their immediate release. "I know how suspicious it sounds," the Killmaster said. "But as you noted yourself, you have to take this all in context. Dr. Zachary is looking desperately for information that will clear his agency from some rather severe and damaging circumstantial evidence." Without mentioning specific names or events, Carter filled Alvarado in on the missing corpse at Covington.

It was difficult to see if Alvarado bought any of this or not. He remained as stoic as some of the Aztec faces on the large murals at the university. "And you, Señor Carter?"

"I am in your country," the Killmaster said, "trying to determine the source, nature, and immediate intent of an organization that appears not to be political but which has a definite military character." Carter spoke a few words on his need to be as discreet as possible about the more specific nature of his mission.

Alvarado smiled for the first time. "Would you say, Señor Carter, that if you were allowed to remain in our country unhindered and you developed all the information you needed, that you would be willing to share the more important aspects of your information?"

Carter did not want to appear too eager. "I need to be discreet, but yes, I would certainly be willing to brief you on the aspects that apply to your country."

Alvarado reached into a drawer and came forth with a large manila file, bulging with papers. He dropped it on the desk with such a crash that Zachary blinked. "This entire folder contains the equivalents of promises from other countries and agencies to share with us." Leafing through the folder at random, he began to name off countries. "England wanted our cooperation on this. Cuba on this one. Ah, here is one from West Germany, and this is from Bulgaria, and this, señores, is from your old friends, the Union of Soviet Socialist Republics. And this is from the United States."

"Okay," Zachary said, "you can drop the other shoe, although I think we both get your point."

"Excellent," Captain Alvarado said, "because a point needs

to be made. All these memos and promises are worthless. I have found out more from reading newspapers than from the men and women who have sat where you two are now sitting, giving me their solemn words."

Carter wanted to ask how many of these persons were still alive, but those implications would only serve to enhance Alvarado's impatience with them.

"Let's return to you for a moment, Señor Carter. In this venture you are now investigating for your country, please be good enough to tell me which country seems to be in a position to benefit."

"That's not how it works," Carter explained. "No one country is gaining anything, but individuals from a number of countries are apparently being stung for sums of money or other items of great worth."

"I'm beginning to get some ideas, señores," Captain Alvarado said. "Mr. Carter, have you any interst in rare books?"

Carter followed the captain's thinking. "Only in the abstract sense," he said. "I have books I value and some of them are first editions, but I wouldn't go out of my way to pick up a rare volume."

"And you, Señor Zachary, your organization has some animosity toward the PLO?"

"When they use terrorism and stealth, take hostages, and refuse to approach the negotiating table."

"Admirable," Captain Alvarado said, his voice rising, the cords in his neck becoming more apparent. "I have two men of great honor here, who are morally opposed to terrorism, ventures by stealth, and unlicensed incursions."

*Here it comes*, Carter thought.

Looking thoughtfully at Carter and Zachary, Alvarado then turned his attention toward the young man who'd been in charge of the company that captured them. *Any moment now, he's going to be asked to leave the room*, Carter speculated. Then the dramatic intensity would increase and later, the young lieutenant would be handed an envelope with cash. No explanation necessary.

Alvarado really began to pour it on, citing the number of unsolved violent deaths that had occurred in Mexico since their arrival. "The fact is that you both take this high-minded posture and yet it is very likely that you are responsible for these mysterious deaths." His dark eyes scanned them. "I do not delude myself. You are both at this very moment calculating how much it is going to take to buy me off. I am aware of the reputation of the Latin American civil servant in that regard. The word is *mordida*. Oh, yes, I've heard it called *propina*, but whether you call it graft or a tip, it still comes to the same thing, and as far as I'm concerned, it does not apply here. But do you gentlemen get my intent?"

He nodded to the young lieutenant. "Please listen to this carefully, *compadre*. I want you to be very clear on all this." Then he pointed a well-manicured hand toward Zachary and Carter. "Just as you are looking at me and wondering how much money it will take to bribe me, I am looking at you and wondering what kind of morals and ethics the two of you have."

"All right," Zachary said, "you're honest and you're not looking for a bribe. What are you looking for?"

"I'm looking for what we all in this profession look for. I want information. Pure and simple. No *mordida*. No *propina*. No donations to the state police retirement fund or whatever other imaginative twist you wish to give it. I want information."

There was a long silence.

"To give you a frame of reference," Alvarado said, "I tell you now that it is already a foregone conclusion that you are going to leave Mexico. Based on the information you give me, your departure will have options. If your information is false, I will see to it that your departure is from a courtroom and that you will be denied bail. If you give me good information, you will be given a ride back to your hotel, and you will have, shall we say thirty-six hours before I come looking for you. Your choice, señores. A prison breakfast, and detention until you appear before the magistrate, or a voluntary retirement from the Republic of Mexico."

Nick Carter smiled. "If an exchange of funds for the privilege of staying in your country cannot be arranged, we have very little other choice left."

Alvarado took his win graciously. "We have reached that plateau. No funds will be exchanged. You have a limited time —a very limited time left in Mexico." He pointedly addressed the lieutenant. "And you? You understand the ethics of this?"

If the young officer was disappointed that any possibility of the exchange of money was now out of the picture, he managed to hide it. Carter was impressed with both of them. Mexico often got a bad rap on its public officials.

Captain Alvarado returned his focus to Carter and Zachary. "Let's begin, señores, with you telling me what you know about an individual named Piet Bezeidenhout."

"Bingo," Zachary said, smiling in triumph. "All of a sudden, Captain Alvarado, I think I have a high regard for you."

The Killmaster smiled as well. He knew exactly what Sam Zachary was thinking.

# TEN

"Thirty-six hours is rather generous, under the circumstances," Margo Huerta said.

Chepe Muñoz was even more emphatic. "That was one fine cop you guys ran into."

Carter said, "It suited his purpose to be lenient. He knew Bezeidenhout was in his country, he was smart enough to know that Sam and I were not your ordinary cops, and he figured we might be on the up and up."

"So what did you tell him, man?" Chepe Muñoz said. "Or maybe I should put it like this: How little did you guys have to tell him?"

They were finishing a buffet lunch that Margo had set out in her studio, and while the men were alternately showering, shaving, catnapping, and eating, Margo herself became busy on the telephone.

"He knows everything we know short of *LT*," Carter said. "I let him think I was a bounty hunter for multinational insurance companies. He thinks I'm after some missing diamonds."

"That's what I needed," Margo said. "That's a perfect edge to get you in."

While the men continued with their eating, Margo made phone calls, wheedled, cajoled, and frankly traded on favors owed her. She came up with a list of three places where Piet Bezeidenhout had been for meetings during his recent visit to Mexico City.

"Robert Silver, out in Coyoacán," she said in triumph. "Silver actually hosted a gathering of wealthy people to hear Bezeidenhout speak." She wrote the address and gave it to

79

Carter. Muñoz drew a man named Porfirio Gaston, a wealthy merchant. Zachary was to see Enrique Benvenidez, an investments broker. Margo wrote directions to each location on sheets of paper and Carter had the distinct impression that the one she dealt him was the one she believed would prove the most profitable.

It was Zachary who first raised the issue that was on all their minds. "Margo, you'd better keep a weapon close at hand from now on. All the people you've been calling are aware of your interest in Bezeidenhout. Any of them or their associates could want you silenced."

"Listen," the fiery Margo said with an arrogant toss of her head, "I've been associated with struggles of one sort or another for years. You think this is the worst danger I've ever been in?"

Without hesitation, all three men nodded.

"All right," she said contritely, "I'll be careful."

While Carter was finishing a large plate of shrimp and rice, Margo cleaned and redressed the handiwork of Dr. Hakluyt on his left shoulder, building in a bit of padding and support. "You listen to me, Carter," she said, sitting herself down on his lap when the taping and bandaging was completed. "You and I—we have unfinished business, you understand? Several days of it?" She stood and tossed Carter a fresh shirt she'd picked up for him.

The Killmaster, Zachary, and Chepe Muñoz set up contingency plans for where they would meet if they could not regroup before Captain Alvarado's thirty-six-hour deadline.

"Seems to me there's only one logical place," the CIA man said, looking approvingly at the remains of the buffet.

Carter, Muñoz, and Zachary agreed, and discussed strategy. "Just in case," Carter said, "we should each memorize the connection given the other two. That way, if one of us fails to return, the others will have a strong clue."

"Strange bedfellows we are," Zachary said. "But it appears we all trust one another."

Chepe Muñoz shook his head in disbelief. "Dr. Castro would have my ass if he knew I was getting on so famously with a couple of capitalists."

Carter nodded at Margo. "Just in case we can't regroup here, you'd better join us at the rendezvous too."

The flamboyant artist liked that very much, and winked conspiratorially at Carter.

Carter was out the door first, noting that Zachary was hurriedly building himself a sandwich to take along.

Nick Carter's next stop was the wealthy suburb of Coyoacán. He stopped to call Hawk and give him the names of all three places Margo Huerta had learned about.

"I'm going in as a member of the South African diamond cartel security."

"Good idea," Hawk said. "Get them to doubt this Bezeidenhout as much as possible without seeming too obvious."

Carter could tell that Hawk was growing impatient with the way the LT activity ws developing. "A bit of an irony in your going out to Coyoacán, Nick. Leon Trotsky lived and was assassinated there. The famed painter, Diego Rivera, lived there. Both are associated with the politics of the left."

There was a pause while Hawk thumbed the wheel of his lighter and puffed at one of his cigars. Then he continued, "Whatever happens, we want to know what Lex Talionis is, what it's doing, and who is behind it. And we want it soon. The pressure on me has become unbelievable. I don't need to tell you where it comes from, either."

Carter quickly found a cab and gave the instructions to Coyoacán, an attractive suburb with numerous parks, broad, cobbled streets, and a sense of quiet, refined good taste.

As in so many large cities where there was a high rate of crime and poverty, the area had its share of high fences, barbed wire, and elaborate security measures.

Following the instructions given him, Carter directed the driver past the Plaza Hidalgo, turned right at the Church of San Juan Bautista, and came upon one of the innumerable streets named after Mexican political or religious martyrs. In this case, it was the street of the child heroes: La Calle de los Niños Héroes.

The Silver home appeared to be only modestly affluent when Carter sounded the bell at a small wrought-iron gate, but he was soon greeted by a servant who had him follow her through a small bricked courtyard and onto a much more lavish lawn that was part of an elaborate tropical garden.

Traveling along a neat gravel path, Carter noted two large,

snarling mastiffs, ready to pounce. He was ushered into a
white stone building with tall, soaring ceilings, a tile floor of
immense complexity, and several large pre-Columbian pieces,
notably a dog that was larger than any pre-Columbian ceramic
animal Carter had ever seen.

"Cortez, the conqueror of Mexico, once had a kingly pal-
ace right here in Coyoacán."

This was said by a short balding man with a large head and
seemingly bulging eyes who then stepped into the foyer and
introduced himself. Shaking hands with Robert Silver, Carter
tried to get some kind of impression of him. For the most part,
it was one of a barely concealed arrogance in a man in his late
forties or early fifties.

"I must tell you that it took a great deal of pressure from
Margo Huerta to induce me to agree to this meeting, Señor
Carter. I am not particularly pleased at your visit. As you will
see when we step inside, I am fond of works of art, Señorita
Huerta's works among them—and I would hardly want to put
myself in a position of having someone whose work I admire
not want me to have any more."

"I understand that I am here at your sufferance," Carter
said in a cultivated monotone. "This is a very delicate matter."

Dressed casually in gray flannels, a white shirt, and a
fawn-colored sweater vest, Silver led the way down a hallway
and into what must have been the man's private study. "At
least you have wit and sensitivity. I can appreciate that, perhaps." He motioned Carter to a large overstuffed club chair
and for himself chose an equally large Eames chair.

A servant came scraping at the door and with her was,
Carter saw immediately, a major reason for Silver's arrogance.
Mrs. Silver was still in her thirties, her tawny complexion,
wide-set dark eyes, and high cheekbones linking her back over
the centuries to the original peoples of Mexico. Unlike Silver,
her Spanish was fluid, melodic Mexican. Her thick dark hair,
if allowed to fall free, would most likely reach her knees,
Carter estimated. He admired the lacquered beauty of it as it
was knotted and braided artfully to display an elegant neck.

Carter felt a strong twinge of desire as her eyes met his,
filled with a different kind of pride than her husband's. She
may indeed be yet another of his fabled possessions, but she
had a luster and determination of her own. As she offered

Carter the choice of Mexican chocolate or coffee and cognac, he could see in the soft light the one anomaly to her otherwise stunning presence. There was a definite trace of a welt beginning to form on her left cheek. It was clear to Carter that Mr. Silver had been responsible and equally clear that Mrs. Silver intended to do something about it. While the servant was preparing the drinks, Silver produced a large ebony cigar box and extended it to Carter. "A great civilized pleasure, the tobacco of our friends in Cuba. As it so often happens, those who produce the civilized pleasures are least likely to enjoy them."

"I take it you have little regard for the Cubans, Mr. Silver." He thought he saw a flicker of amusement from Mrs. Silver.

"It depends what your historical thrust is, Carter. That bearded idiot is not one of my favorites."

"Even so," Carter said, "there are those who say Dr. Castro is greatly preferable to the late General Batista."

Silver grew impatient, which was what Carter wanted. "But of course, the reason for your being here is to discuss politics, eh, Carter?" The balding little man still did not betray a country or language of origin. His English was flat, nasal, correct; he might easily have gone to an English school or studied the language at an elite school for English diplomats' children somewhere abroad.

Mrs. Silver crossed her legs demurely. It was not by any account a provocative gesture, but her physical beauty and her seemingly great reserves of dignity touched Carter.

Silver didn't miss Carter's attraction to his wife. "Yes," Silver said. "Consuela is a great treasure. One could almost call her a national treasure. She is certainly worth a good deal."

After the maid returned with drinks, Carter noticed that Silver spoke to her in a flawless Spanish with Mexican accents and intonations. He dismissed the maid, then in English dismissed Mrs. Silver. Carter watched her go with great reluctance.

"May I add to my impertinence at being here by asking you your profession, Mr. Silver?"

Silver used a wooden match to fire a cherry-red glow to the tip of his cigar. The fragrant tobacco made Carter salivate. He wished David Hawk had such tastes. "I am a diamond merchant, Carter."

Carter played on the man's vanity. "Yes, we know about that."

Silver's left brow twitched in response. "There was a time when I was a diamond cutter, and I must say I was a rather gifted one, being an apprentice of my late uncle, one of the great European diamond cutters. But as in all things in this life, Carter, art is not enough. A diamond cutter can live well, but not so well as this." He spread his hand to indicate the shelves, laden with artifacts of turquoise, jade, obsidian, and ceramic. "Not with things in his house that once belonged to the great Hernan Cortez, eh?"

"Is that how you know Piet Bezeidenhout?"

"Right to the point, eh? You ask purposeful questions, Carter. Are you a lawyer?"

Carter shook his head, then sipped his cognac. He was letting Silver's curiosity build.

"Ah, then, some other kind of professional, eh?" He showed Carter a wide grin filled with irony and a great deal of costly dental work. "I think it only fair that you tell me what you do. Señorita Huerta suggested you have something to do with diamonds."

"As you know, sir, the diamond cartel has a security force. Piet Bezeidenhout is a high-ranking member." He paused to drop his bomb. "I, too, am a high-ranking member of that organization."

Carter watched Silver's reaction. He was guardedly curious.

"All right. Since I have agreed to discuss the matter with you, let us begin, eh? Allow me to anticipate your first question: Piet Bezeidenhout was in this house two weeks ago with a gathering of perhaps twelve others."

Puffing leisurely on his cigar, Robert Silver told of meeting Piet Bezeidenhout when he was learning the diamond trade in Brussels. The Afrikaner seemed always to have an eye for works of art that increased in value. Equally, he was always interested in the pleasures of the dining room and, of course, the bedroom.

When Silver was transferred to Amsterdam to begin grading diamonds and actually marking the better stones for cutting by the top cutters, Bezeidenhout appeared again from time to time, and while Silver would not want to say they were fast friends, nevertheless, one becomes bonded to a person one has gone out drinking, dining, and whoring with over a period of time.

"And so," Carter said, "as Bezeidenhout grew in power with the diamond security police, he began spending more time away from Johannesburg and Capetown and more time abroad, making sure the interests of the diamond cartel were strictly upheld. The two of you probably had occasion to meet in places like Paris, Rome, Antwerp, New York, and Beverly Hills, eh?"

Silver watched Carter carefully.

Using his excellent memory, Carter went on describing Bezeidenhout to Silver just as Bezeidenhout had been described to him in the dispatches left for him back in the private jet that had taken him from Toronto to Phoenix. The effect on Silver was unsettling.

"Why are his own people so interested in him all of a sudden?" Silver asked.

Carter made it a rule not to let someone he was interrogating take over the questioning. "Why do you think we're interested?"

"He is a headstrong man. He has his own beliefs."

"We are also headstrong," Carter persisted. "What did he talk about when he was last here, in this place?"

Robert Silver furrowed his brow and swirled his cognac. "You want everything, eh, Carter? Piet spoke of the growing difficulties of protecting personal investments or fortunes. He reminded some of us that the same is growing true in Mexico as well. It is becoming more and more difficult to use barricades, fences, and barbed wire to keep out the poor. Do you have any idea how many there are here in the capital alone?"

"This is what he talked about? The poor?"

"He talked about the need to keep incentives alive for those who were intersted in advancing their goals of security."

"Why do I have the feeling that you're speaking in generalities, Mr. Silver?"

Silver took a large toss of his cognac. "Ah, yes, you would like it if I told you that Piet was talking about apartheid and perhaps even the purity of races. You'd like that, eh, Carter?" He stood abruptly. "Well, I'm not going to give you that. Piet is a businessman, not an ideologue. He was here discussing business."

"You understand that his business is our business?"

"Dammit, Carter, you go too far as it is. He did not discuss the diamond business."

Carter was sure his time in the big house was coming to an end. "Did he extend an offer to you, Mr. Silver?"

"That was your last question, Carter, and the answer is yes, he extended an offer to me and to all the others. I will have you shown out now. I have been more than hospitable. I have no idea what you will make of this or how you will proceed, but you leave with more than when you came and so my conscience is clear."

"So is your devotion to Bezeidenhout," Carter said. "You should be careful in your dealings with him."

"Is that a warning, Mr. Carter, or just an observation?"

The Killmaster met him eye to eye. "A warning," he said. A moment later the maid came to see him to the main gate.

Carter headed for the square and a taxi back to the Zocalo, deciding that Silver had been disturbed by his questions. This probe had touched something tender.

He'd gone only a block or so when he had the feeling of movement behind him and turned to note a cream-white Mercedes with tinted windows slowly moving toward him, drawing abreast of him, then stopping. The door on the passenger side was pushed open.

Consuela Silver had looked demure and elegant seated in her husband's den. There was nothing demure about her now, the angle of the seat and the driving pedals causing her full skirt to fall back over her trim legs, revealing knees and thighs. She was aware of Carter's admiration but made no move to tug her skirt down. "I need to talk to you, Señor Carter." There was an edge in her voice that Carter could not read. "In private."

He got into the Mercedes and sat beside her. She drove to the large Coyoacán plaza and parked in the darkness near a group of ancient pepper trees.

"I like it very much that you find me attractive, Señor Carter. There is nothing furtive about you, certainly nothing like—" She stopped for a moment, biting thoughtfully at her lower lip.

"This is not what you think, Señor Carter. At least not all of it. I am more than a bored housewife who for too long has become an object of possession and display." She ran a finger over her left cheek. "As you can no doubt tell, my husband and I had a disagreement that came to violence." She looked into his eyes. "I am not one of these long-suffering women who allows such insults. This is the first time Robert has ever struck me. If he were not such an inherently corrupt, evil man, I would be content merely to do what I am about to do, and then leave him. Your visit tonight is very symbolic for me." Her eyes played over him, first with sympathy, then with open invitation. She seemed to be taking in Carter's appreciation of her and encouraging it.

"I know who you are," she said. "I don't really know the details, the exact details, but I know you have some large power behind you, that you are a survivor and a fighter. Robert actually thinks you represent the diamond security forces." She laughed. "I know you represent reason and compassion, that you have probably had to kill for those qualities, and that you have had your life in peril on more occasions than you care to remember."

Carter felt himself pulled along by the strength of her presence and convictions. She watched him for a time, then reached for his hand, squeezed it first, then began tracing the back of it with her fingertips. "Does that arouse you, Señor Carter?"

"Everything about you arouses me," Carter admitted.

She made a small humming noise of satisfaction. "That is truly good fortune for me. My husband and his friends, they are aroused by the sight of things, but for them the true excitement is possession. Their imaginations stop with possession. Do you understand the implications of that? Always being looked at as an object, always being possessed but never appreciated?"

Consuela Silver placed Carter's hand on her bare thigh. The warmth of her skin made him catch his breath, and she was obviously pleased by his reaction. "There are many things we can do for one another, Señor Carter, things that go well beyond mere possession. That great fool of a man wanted me because of my family lineage. My family is not wealthy now, although at one time they were. Now it is more the tradition of trying to lead a good life, a life where the tradition and dignity prevail. It was thought that my husband was a decent man and that I would be able to carry on the tradition of doing good things for the benefit of all."

By now she was facing him, and she pulled him toward her.

Carter felt the pleasure of having his face buried against the side of that remarkably graceful neck, his hands moving slightly to cup the swell of her elegant breasts.

She shuddered at his touch. "I did not think it was possible to have such exquisite pleasures from these little explorations. Explore me, Señor Carter. Go wherever your pleasure takes you. Tell me what you enjoy."

She made intimate moves along the sides of Carter's thighs. He responded immediately. Her eyes lit with an animal excitement. The results goaded Carter on. He continued his exploration of her breasts. She hummed in pleasure. "There is this other thing I have spoken of. We must make love right here and that will give me the energy I need to do this other thing."

"Sounds very dramatic," Carter murmured.

Gravely, deliberately, Consuela Silver nodded. She moistened her lips, then straddled Carter's lap. "You must make love to me now and then I shall go home and kill my husband."

# ELEVEN

Carter felt a chill and a surge of passion at the same time. He did not know Consuela Silver, but just as she had felt a kinship with him, so did he know her well enough to know she meant what she'd said.

As if reading his thoughts, she said, "I am quite serious. If it had merely been that he lost control and hit me, you and I would not be here like this now. I am not doing this to get revenge on him or, how do you say it, put the horns on him. I do this to purge myself of a truly evil presence in my life."

She began to make it difficult for him to concentrate on anything but her. The gentleness of her touch and her obvious desire to make this a shared experience overrode any thought Carter might have had at being merely a part of some insensitive individual's personal sexual ritual.

After several moments, Consuela Silver began whispering questions to him, telling him places where she wanted him to touch her, then taking his hands and guiding them to her breasts, her legs, her hips, and beyond. "You know this was what you wanted from the moment you saw me," she said.

Then she kissed him hungrily. "It's true, this is what you wanted, and you made me want it too." She closed her eyes and sighed. "I didn't think you were ever going to get out of there so we could be doing this."

"This is something I want," Carter whispered.

Before he could respond, she nodded and smiled. "Yes," she said, "I know what you want." She pulled two tortoise shell pins from her hair and the long twists and braids of it came tumbling down, splashing over her face and shoulders.

Her mocha-colored skin was bathed in the glistening silkiness of that heavy raven hair.

His hands played over her body, enjoying the feel of her waist, her hips, her powerful legs. Soon she whispered a specific request to him. "Please!" she breathed. And Carter unbuttoned her blouse and began to softly caress her breasts, causing her to close her eyes and groan.

All the while Carter was caressing her, she was busy with him, making it possible for their bodies to join. As they did, Carter felt her stiffening momentarily and then, almost immediately, the complete giving of herself to their lovemaking. "You are the first man other than my husband," she said. "He had suggested others—other things, but you are the first. I have chosen well."

As Carter began to control their movements, Consuela cried out several times, her back arching. Then, her hands digging at his neck and shoulders, she said, "I want you, now, then I will be complete."

Although Carter still tried to be in control, her movements and the great sense of being joined to so intense and attractive a person became more than he could endure.

"Please!" she cried. "Now!"

She whispered surprising things in Carter's ear, moving with a frenzy that brought him to the state she wanted. As Carter experienced the pure, driving response of excitement, he was aware of her being raised one more time to that point herself.

For some time she held him tightly, caressing him as the full sensation swept over both of them. Once again it seemed to Carter that Consuela had been with him every moment of their lovemaking, that she was one of the most responsive women he'd ever known.

After a time in the dark car, her voice seemed to come from a distance. "This has been very important to me. I do not know what will happen to me or where I will go after I leave you and do what I must, but no matter what, you have made me understand things that will stay with me and comfort me."

Even when she gently lifted herself from atop him and sat for a moment, she reached for him and touched his face gently, continuing the intimacy.

"Bezeidenhout is a completely amoral man," she said. "He

must be stopped. My husband and some of his friends have put up money. I do not know the exact details, but when I was in the room with all of them, I heard this pig of a man speaking of what he called the sensible solution. If a few innocent people are caught by them, it is of no matter, they were most likely the sort of people who were natural victims in any case. He spoke of a natural order of things. He spoke of Charles Darwin, and Malthus, and Friedreich Nietzsche."

Carter could feel his blood begin to rush. Why was it that people who spoke of these great men of ideas and beliefs almost invariably did so incorrectly, attaching their own meanings and justifying their own pilosophies?

"Did he," Carter asked, "speak of LT, the law of the lion?"

Consuela nodded. "He spoke of that, and when I looked at my husband, there was an expression on his face that I have tried for years to achieve in a loving way. Not once did he ever respond to me the way he responded to the words and concepts of Piet Bezeidenhout. I have come to realize that my husband and his friends have become completely amoral. The word corrupt no longer applies."

He lit a cigarette and shared it with Consuela.

"Anything else? A place, maybe? Some little detail. I use everything."

"Yes! I forgot. Bezeidenhout mentioned an arts festival in Belize. Run by an American, I believe." He could feel her anger and outrage mounting. "Those men have gone beyond mere accumulation of material wealth. Even more than power, they are attracted to the belief that their sense of justice is of great importance." She took the cigarette from Carter and inhaled. "Their awareness of justice is as remote from real justice as military music is from the work of a man like Bach."

Carter rolled down his window to let in some of the night scents, the perfume of jasmine, frangipani, and gardenia.

When the cigarette was done, she took his face in her hands and gave him a lingering kiss.

She began to button her blouse and for a few moments they laughed at the contortions of her getting back into her skirt, finding her underthings, and locating one of her sandals that had become lost. One of the tortoiseshell pins had fallen from the dashboard to the floor and when they felt along the matting for it, their hands touched and they both experienced another electric moment.

Slowly, almost sadly, Consuela pulled away and began twisting and knotting her hair, pinning it in place.

"I would like to give you this," she said, "as a souvenir of what we have found in each other." She pressed a small round piece of jade into his hand, smaller, thinner than an American dime. Even in the dimness of the car, he could see the piece being like the foamy, clear ocean, green, inviting.

They did not speak again.

She left Carter at a taxi stand.

Back at his hotel, Carter checked the room carefully to see if anyone other than a maid had been poking around. He carefully swept the room for bugs, picked up the telephone, and dialed a series of digits that would cause any tape-recording device to pick up a long, high-pitched tone and little else. Satisfied that the room was clean, he made a final check on invading lasers, then kicked off his shoes and began shucking off his pants while dialing Margo Huerta's number.

"Checking in according to plan," he said without mentioning her name or his. "Mission completed. It appears we're on the right track. In all likelihood, the one I saw is no longer among the living by now. You might check the morning papers."

"Suicide?" Margo said.

"That's a negative," Carter told her.

"It's been a busy night," Margo reported. Using the Mexican expression for "the big fellow," by which she meant Sam Zachary, she said, "El Grandote has reported in as well and confirms your findings. He also brings the news that our other colleague has been taken."

"A trap?" Carter asked.

"Yes. El Grandote used the word *setup*."

"I see," Carter said.

He was about to hang up, but Margo exploded: "They made a big mistake in doing this. They forgot that I know them. They have compromised me, but I'll get them for this."

"Be very careful," Carter cautioned her. "They may not have forgotten at all. They may be planning something for you even now."

He ran a hot shower and got in, letting the water ease the fatigue that had invaded him. He knew there'd be more fatigue up ahead. At the very least, he'd have to spend some time watching Margo's place, just to make sure no one did make a try to get to her.

The thirty-six-hour deadline for leaving Mexico began to look better to him. Things were definitely growing hot and explosive in this country.

Running the needle spray over his aching body, he realized he'd begun to admire Chepe Muñoz. The burly Cuban had style. But there was very little you could do when someone following the same goals as you became a fatality in the line of some enquiry. You found yourself using words or expressions to minimize the death. Chepe was taken out. Chepe bought it. Chepe's number finally came up.

You could vow to make it up for such a person, and even if that smacked of things like revenge or, in this case, the law of the lion, so be it: someone would pay for setting up Muñoz.

He toweled himself dry, managed to rig a clean dressing for his shoulder, and found a cotton turtleneck and some clean trousers. On the way to Margo Huerta's, he bought a large container of coffee and moved along the street until he found a good vantage point, then sat, sipping the hot brew.

He shifted his mind into a focus where he could spot anything unusual, any furtive movements, any attempts to get at Margo's apartment.

Margo's lights went out shortly after midnight and Carter finished the last swallow of coffee about half an hour later.

In this part of Mexico City, things never shut down completely. There was still traffic, and people were still out on the streets. It was essentially a twenty-four-hour city. From time to time a stray noise or movement would engage his attention and he would watch until satisfied that what he'd seen was merely a random part of the street life.

The coffee held him until nearly one-thirty, then he began to feel waves of drowsiness overtake him.

At about two, Carter was alerted by movement behind him. He jerked awake, aware that he'd been dozing for a while. He quickly stood and prepared for an attack.

Sam Zachary stepped out of the shadows, holding a newspaper and a paper cup of coffee. "My turn. You've been on long enough. The watch changes officially at two."

Carter stayed long enough to have a cigarette and get Zachary's details about Chepe Muñoz.

"I got through with my interview after an hour or so and thought I'd stop by and check on Chepe since I was more or less in the neighborhood," the CIA man said. "I had no real reason to worry except that I was met with a lot of hostility and it made me suspicious. Three of them—whoever they were—went in shortly after I arrived, and about half an hour later, they came out carrying a rolled-up rug. I know I have a vivid imagination, but somehow I just couldn't believe that those men were rug cleaners."

"Were you able to follow them?" Carter asked.

"They had a car and I didn't. They lost me, and it appears we lost the Cuban."

The Killmaster ground his cigarette on the pavement.

"You might want to have a look at this," Zachary said, handing him the early-morning edition of the English-language newspaper. The front page bore a headline, *L.A. Shopping Center Rocked by Blast*. The story went on to describe damage caused to stores, parking structures, and escalators in the Beverly Center at Beverly and La Cienega in the northwest part of the city. According to the story, there were only minor injuries sustained by less than half a dozen persons, but the damage to property was listed as close to half a million dollars. Investigators were said to be trying to determine the cause of the explosion. At the moment, the thought was that the explosion was the result of a broken gas main.

"My people," Zachary said, "believe the cause of the explosion was a powerful bomb, carefully placed in a maintenance room. You might want to try David Hawk and see what he's got on it. But I'll bet you a first-rate dinner that it was no accident and had nothing whatever to do with a broken gas main. L.A. is doing something to cover the source because they don't want to mess with the tourist season and they don't want to become the first American city of consequence to be the victim of terrorist activity."

"Sounds like our friends are trying to make a name for themselves and show what they can do," Carter mused.

"Show who?" Zachary said. "That's what we've got to find out."

"The world, I think." Carter took a sip of Zachary's coffee. "Instead of advertising in the *Yellow Pages*, our friends in LT are advertising in heavily populated cities of North America."

# TWELVE

They were sitting in Margo Huerta's apartment when Carter noticed the police car pull up outside.

It was a VW squareback. Hard to miss. He looked at his watch. "Alvarado," he said, "reminding us our time is up. Besides, I'm convinced the trail leads us to Belize. Samadhi seems interested in Rogan, and it looks to me like some cultural festival could be a great cover for something as large as LT. It sounds like an ideal way to get people in from all over the world without causing the slightest suspicion. I wouldn't be surprised to find Bezeidenhout down there. Even if we weren't under the gun from Alvarado, I'd want to be there."

"Sounds right on the money," Zachary said, "but technically we do have a few hours left and I'd like to track those people who got Chepe." He looked at Carter. "You mind?"

"No," Carter said. "I'll let Alvarado take me now. I'll go to Belize and start looking around for traces of LT. Meet you both there. In the beginning, it might be helpful if we pretend not to know each other."

"I can pick up a volunteer job down there," Margo said. "I can infiltrate the staff and see what that brings us."

Carter stood up, impatient. "I want to get on with this. Belize it is." He nodded to Zachary. "I'll buy you some time with Alvarado. See you down there." They arranged to meet either at Belize City or in Belmopan.

He walked down the stairway, strolled out onto the street, and approached the vehicle.

Alvarado pushed the door open for him. "Just one of you?" he paused. "Okay, fair enough. There are a few hours left and

I can see where you might not have had time for all your business. But you're the big one and I'll settle for that as a starter." He looked at his watch. "Zachary has three hours and his ass is out of here."

He drove directly to the airport.

"Do I have to come in with you?"

Carter shook his head.

"In that case, I'll come as a friend." Alvarado handed Carter his weapons. "Here. You'll probably feel more comfortable with your own stuff."

Carter carefully fitted himself with Wilhelmina and Hugo. Pierre took more effort in the car, but Alvarado seemed patient, close to friendly.

"Keep in touch if you learn something," Alvarado said, handing Carter an envelope that contained Carter's passport and a photo of Piet Bezeidenhout. With that, he led Carter over to a money-changing counter. "Get rid of all your Mexican money here. The exchange from peso to Belize dollars always works against you. Besides, you're not going to need pesos anymore. Not for a long time."

As Carter started toward the boarding area, Alvarado moved alongside and conversationally produced a copy of the morning newspaper.

A major front-page story told of the death of Robert Silver, a noted diamond merchant and contributor to political causes.

Carter scanned the details. "I don't see the cause of death listed."

"The cause of death was blunt force trauma, dammit, and don't play with me. I know you were there last night, Carter. I even know you let him believe you were with the diamond cartel security force. That couldn't have anything to do with his death, could it?"

The Killmaster regarded him carefully. Alvarado would not have let him get this close to leaving Mexico if he had truly meant to detain him.

"At the moment, it's a matter of honor that I tell you nothing, Alvarado. But if more than two weeks pass and you have no information, it will be a matter of honor that I tell you what I know."

Alvarado smiled. "The lady's that strong, eh, Carter?"

There was nothing to hold Carter. He went to the boarding gate for the flight departing for Belize City, Belize.

The country of Belize is a small chunk of forest and swamp in the north, jungles and mountains in the south. The yearly rainfall in the south is nearly a hundred inches. As if to make up for this, the north is frequently pounded by hurricanes.

Despite the climate and terrain, the people who come here to stay are fiercely loyal to it. It is an easy, almost idyllic life-style along the coast, more entrepreneurial toward the more temperate central areas. As a culture, it is a healthily mixed bag.

Largely an agricultural country, Belize produces mahogany, fruits and vegetables, and chicle, an essential ingredient in chewing gum. Some of the best *chicleros* or chicle gatherers in the world are from Belize. Not a lot to recommend it, but don't expect disparaging remarks from the people who live there. Expect instead a kind of surprised, laid-back attitude that is often a cover-up for a strong work ethic.

The Guatemalans want it, claiming it was once theirs in the first place; the Belezians want it, claiming it has its own culture and habits; the British administer it, although not conspicuously, and like the idea of still having a place in that part of the world.

The ethnic mixture in Belize is striking, with a number of Caribbean peoples, indigenous Indians, colonials, Europeans, and North Americans.

The airport was surprisingly large. Someone was expecting lots of big planes to land. Perhaps it was the optimism of a small, underdeveloped country, and perhaps there was something else going on. A number of signs gave a sense of activity. One said the new capital city in Belmopan would soon be the most beautiful and sophisticated in Central America. Another welcomed people of artistry and imagination from all over the world to the Festival of the Arts at the Belize Center for the Arts. Yet another warned newcomers that now was the time to get their Belize auto insurance.

The climate was humid and oppressive. Taking a cab from the airport, Carter gave the driver a big tip and was given an orientation tour of the city. The driver, an agreeable and handsome Carib with a mahogany complexion, told Carter he'd lived in Belize City most of his life. His license and identity photo listed him as Julius Sortero.

"Except I done some time in Chicago, boss," Julius Sortero said. "I make big money and come back here and buy into dese here taxis. I got four working for me and two, three junker cars at me house for spare parts."

The driver went to a large movable bridge spanning a creek large enough to float a huge boat. "Dis called Swing Bridge, an' it the major place in town as you can see wid your own eyes. It go over Haulover Creek, make plenty room for boats and barges to pass through. Dis the closest thing we got to a monument." But Julius Sortero also pointed out the high contrast between the ramshackle, slapdash way of life along the coast and some of the more exotic and substantial buildings and homes, reminiscent of the British colonial influence, but also reflecting modern architecture. Colors of homes and buildings ranged from the durable whitewash to bright blues, subdued orange, and sophisticated grays.

In several areas in downtown Belize City, Carter saw signs announcing that the huge arts center in nearby Belmopan was having a Festival of the Arts. James Rogan's name was connected with it.

Carter was set to check in at the Fort George Hotel, but Julius took his role as guide seriously and took him over to Regent Street and stopped in front of the Hotel Mopan. "You might suspect I get a cut of the take if I bring you here, but I do dis out of my own conviction that you don' want no tourist trap."

Carter took Julius at his word, paid him, and booked a room. He'd checked his weapons at the airport but wanted to go through them at more leisure. The room was an ideal place for it.

Armed and rigged for action, Carter set out to start bringing in useful information and find himself a rental car so that he could get going.

There were a number of adobe buildings, wooden sheds, and some attempts at stucco work in varying degrees, but when Carter found the Central Park, he began to see signs of ambitious building, major department stores, boutiques, old, colonial-style buildings, a movie theater, and several bars with a straightforward Caribbean ambience on the outside, a hybrid of reggae, Willie Nelson, and Billy Joel on the inside. A block away he saw a sign, SMITH AND SONS AUTO RENTAL. After some negotiations he was given a car that sounded acceptable, but when he checked it out, he came back inside the rental office. "I want a car I can rely on," he said. "I'm willing to pay for it."

"Where you be going?" the frightened clerk asked.

"Belmopan, more or less."

"I do have a Toyota with some oomph to it."

"I'll take it," Carter said.

"Can't let you do that, not for three, four hours. It surely be back then, and we'll say you got it reserved."

Carter took himself to the Upstairs Café, where he saw a number of posters and advertisements for the Belize Center for the Written and Performing Arts, some already dated, announcing that James Rogan was giving poetry readings or discussions of the classics.

He entered, looked around the well-lit room, and almost immediately the sound of a brief scuffle broke out at one of the rear tables. Carter was aware of someone leaving in a hurry. Someone who had not wanted to be seen? Carter wondered.

Carter was down the stairs immediately. The man wore a shirt with rolled-up sleeves. Running shoes. Olive drab pants. Out on the street, he started running toward the Swing Bridge, Carter not far behind. Seeing that Carter was getting close, the man angled across a small park where some old people had set up a vegetable and fruit stand. The quarry put on a burst of speed as Carter began gaining, then managed to vanish in a row of dilapidated shacks. But Carter had a good idea who hadn't wanted to be seen. Abdul Samadhi.

Carter returned to the Upstairs Café and looked carefully at the table where Samadhi had sat. A group of four men, possibly Arabs, sat glaring at him. Carter stood at the edge of the table. "Tell your friend," he said in Arabic, "that I will wring his scrawny neck when I catch him."

The four at the table made no response.

"Did you hear me?" Carter snapped.

Sullenly, the men began to eat.

Carter grabbed one of the men by the arm and twisted so that he was forced off his chair onto his knees. The other three were on their feet. "Did you hear me?" Carter demanded.

The one on the floor nodded.

"You have bad manners," Carter said. "All of you."

The men returned to their meal. No one else in the café responded, but Carter hadn't expected any of them to know Arabic. He chose a table by himself and looked at the menu. The Upstairs Café had two menus, the bean-and-fish-oriented dishes that went with the Caribbean culture, and a more traditional American menu of hamburgers, stews, fried chicken, pies, and soft drinks.

Carter settled on the chicken and began to notice groups of men at various tables, some of them Caucasian, possibly European from their dress, some blacks, and a few Latinos. From time to time the men at the table from which Samadhi had fled looked over at Carter with cold menace.

A noisy clatter erupted downstairs. Carter guessed it was a bus, trying to start.

By the time Carter's chicken was served, a rather shaggy-looking man, tall, slightly bent at the shoulders, some gray in his longish hair, came into the room and approached one of the tables of men. He wore khakis and field boots. Wire-rimmed glasses were perched on his nose. A name patch read Unkefer, D., but there were no other insignia to show a military or civilian affiliation. "Any of you turkeys know diesel engines?"

The men regarded him in a friendly enough manner, but no one spoke.

Unkefer went to the next table and spoke in German, adding a number of colloquialisms and regionalisms when he spoke.

One of the men told Unkefer he could handle a Mercedes. Unkefer actually took a piece of chicken from the man's plate and chewed it for a moment. "The only way a guy like you would get near a Mercedes is to steal it."

The others laughed, but once again, Unkefer was forced farther afield to find someone, even stopping at Carter's table and asking him. Carter noted that Unkefer addressed him in English, and he marveled at the newcomer's ability to choose the first language of so many of the men in the room.

Carter nodded and agreed to go downstairs with Unkefer. There was a bus parked below and two men were working at it with mounting frustration.

Carter peered in, familiarizing himself with the layout and condition of the large engine. "This isn't the original engine for this bus," he said.

A tall, swarthy man standing next to Unkefer snarled, "We aren't asking for a pedigree, just a hand in getting the mother to run."

Unkefer nudged him. "Easy, man," he said. "This guy's helping us, remember?"

"Yeah, well, he don't have to go nosing around."

"Actually, it's quite an imaginative job of cannibalized parts," Carter said. "I see some English parts, some German parts, some Brazilian parts, and these parts over here are clearly Russian."

"Wiseguy," the swarthy one said. "What's that supposed to mean?"

Unkefer appeared to have lost his patient cool. "Will you can it?" He moved in front of the swarthy man and pushed him aside. To Carter he said, "No offense. Thanks for your efforts."

After ten minutes of fiddling, Carter settled on checking the water-to-fuel regulator and the spark coil. At a call from Carter, the driver turned over the engine, which lugged for a few turns, cranked precariously, then caught hold.

Unkefer was delighted. "Let me buy you a beer, man. Hell, let me pay for your lunch."

Carter waved away the gesture in a friendly manner that would not offend. "Where are you headed?"

"Right outside Belmopan."

"Ah, the arts center?"

"You know it?" Unkefer asked.

"I heard Rogan give a big reading at the university in Mexico City."

"Yeah, well, if that stuff interests you, man, you should come out and visit. All kinds of classes and stuff out there."

Carter smiled.

He returned to the restaurant, washed, and ate his chicken. In another few minutes, Unkefer appeared, rounded up all the men who had been glaring at Carter, and sent a beer over to Carter's table.

There was a connection between these people and Samadhi and the Center for the Arts. Not only that, Carter's arrival in Belize was marked. People knew he was here now. The character of the restaurant changed immediately when the groups of men were gone and loaded into the bus below. A few Belizian postal employees lingered over their meals, and clusters of tourists consulted the menus or ate the large, savory portions set before them by agreeable Carib women who worked as waitresses.

The policy at the Upstairs Café was for second helpings of yams, beans, potatoes, and greens. Carter suspected there could be thirds as well for those who had the room.

Calling over his waitress, Carter asked, "Do you know anything about those men who were here before?"

She looked about nervously, and lowered her voice. "Dis part of the world, dere ain't as much to be particular about as in your part of the world. People come to get jobs as *chicleros*, milking them chicle trees. Sometimes they be a roundup to do some felling of the mahogany trees. I hear they pay good wages. And over to Belmopan, they be pavin' roads and puttin' up buildings to make the new capital. Lots of work a man could do—if he keep his eyes open."

"What's your opinion about where that last group was going?" Carter pushed a few American dollars toward her. Nervously, she picked up the bills.

"They sure wasn't no *chicleros*, because men what does that, they got a pungent odor about them, being out there an' all. I'd say they maybe could be your construction types, lookin' to make big money in the long-term construction projects."

Carter pushed two more dollars toward her. "You say maybe. And maybe they're something else."

Her eyes rolled. "Sometimes lately, seems to me a lot come through here wantin' to play soldier."

"Where do they go? Do they stay here in Belize?" He shoved a five at her.

"Man, how do I know where dey all go? I cannot take dat fiver."

"Take it," Carter said. "It's okay."

She looked about her uneasily. "You telling me you gonna protect me from now on?"

"What do you need to be protected from?"

"Man, some folks say the ones who like to play soldier, they end up in places like Honduras or Nicaragua, learnin' a trade." There was a heavy irony lacing her voice.

"What kind of trade?"

"Man, they become magicians." She gave a nervous laugh and lowered her face toward Carter's. "You know what I mean? They learn how to take people who ask too many questions and make 'em disappear."

Carter pushed the five at her. "You've earned it," he said. He decided to walk off the effects of the heavy meal. At a magazine stand he bought a small map of the area, noticing with interest the range of periodicals and magazines. There were the omnipresent comic books in Spanish and English, there was a stack of old *National Geographic* magazines for a Belize dollar apiece, the international edition of *Newsweek*, and an entire section of *Soldier of Fortune* magazines, some over two years old. There was a large stack of the latest edition as well. Equally imposing were the displays of handgun- and rifle-oriented magazines, priced in Belize dollars according to their newness.

He checked his watch. He still had two hours before he could have the rental car. He made the rounds of bars and coffee shops, and saw one place where he noted guns and ammunition were sold. He was looking for traces of Samadhi. His cohorts had undoubtedly gone on that bus with Unkefer, but maybe the cocky PLO man was still in town.

When he found no trace of Samadhi, Carter walked back to the Hotel Mopan, secured his room, and settled down for a nap. It could be a long time before he had a good sleep again.

It was still light when he awakened. He showered and went down into the bar for some coffee. After two cups and a cinnamon bun, Carter felt measurably better and went out and found a dry goods store where he bought a serviceable pair of chinos, a lightweight chambray work shirt, and a flop-brimmed straw hat to wear against the ravages of the tropical sun. He went back to the car rental place and told them he'd expect the car in half an hour. No excuses. It was time to move.

Back at the hotel, he packed, left coded messages for Zachary and Margo Huerta, checked out, and loaded his things in the car.

The rental car was a Toyota from the early '80s. Scratched and dented here and there, it nevertheless had reliable tread on the tires and a good response to the gas pedal. Carter filled the tank at a station near the Swing Bridge, put in an hour driving around, still looking for traces of Abdul Samadhi, then headed into the late afternoon sun, away from the coastal humidity and onward toward Belmopan.

The Western Highway to Belmopan was about as good a road as Carter had seen in a developing country. While not luxuriously wide in some places on a steep upgrade, nevertheless there were wide shoulders on either side and, in a few places, turnouts to allow slower traffic to pull over safely if a faster driver wanted to pass.

There were some potholes, but there were also signs that a road crew had recently been through doing some patching work. The road took Carter roughly southwest, into the foothills of the Maya Mountains and through farming country that was colorful and inviting. Carter made excellent time; darkness had just begun to set in as he noticed a sign for the cutoff to Belmopan.

Signs of civilization were apparent almost immediately, but some of them reminded Carter of real estate developments he'd seen in various desert and mountain areas. Signs and staked-out areas began to abound, a number of well-articulated foundations were dug, and yet others had been poured, with piles of equipment set nearby. A series of signs spoke of the Belmopan twenty-year plan, and another, lit by a modern mercury vapor lamp, told of the pride with which Belezians could view their new country capital.

Carter drove past a few scattered farms, a small shantytown, and a more ambitious series of housing tracts, surrounded by a wide, well-paved ring road.

Continuing south, Carter found a business area with gas stations, a few groceries and a feed and grain store, all closed for the day. Several hundred yards away another clump of activity seemed well lit in the mountainous night, and Carter saw another gas station, a few garages, food shops, and a modest inn with hand-painted signs and numerous flowerpots filled with geraniums.

He also noted two banks, a post office, a large and neat-looking hospital, and the large pink cinder-block building with enormous dish antennas on the roof, a microwave telephone installation. That meant he could check in at the AXE nerve center and talk to David Hawk.

Driving on, Carter saw another of the ubiquitous signs, this less ambitious and cruder than the others: BELIZE CENTER FOR THE ARTS, 10 KMS. Six miles to the south. The sign contained information in English and Spanish about the Spring Festival of the Arts.

Carter parked and approached the inn, thinking to find a beer and a room. If Zachary were on schedule, he should be there.

He had no sooner entered the lobby when a familiar voice greeted him. "Just in time for a nightcap, Carter. I'm buying." Sam Zachary lifted a glass in salute.

# THIRTEEN

They sat in the small café area, drinking beer. "I think I had a run-in with Samadhi," Carter said. "In Belize City. He took off. Lost me. But there's a lot of activity around here that validates our suspicions. I'm pushing to get out to that arts center. I just know that there's a connection between Samadhi and the LT that we're not seeing and I won't rest until I get it."

Zachary ran through his experiences before leaving Mexico City. "I went to see the people Chepe Muñoz interviewed. They swore they didn't turn him in. They said there'd been people watching their home since Bezeidenhout had been there."

"You believed that?" Carter asked.

"I pressed them, and got them to tell me what Bezeidenhout had talked to their group about. I got stuff that backs up your theory, Carter. Bezeidenhout was trying to sell shares in an organization that would become a multinational political arm, beholden to no one. They intend to work it like a law firm: you've got the money to pay their fees, they're on your side and won't sell you out to another client."

Carter's anger dropped a notch. The story made a grim kind of sense. "It's like paying a yearly retainer fee for terrorism."

"Son of a bitch," Zachary said, standing. "When you put it that way, the hell with sleep. Let's go."

"You might as well grab a few hours. I've got an errand and it may take me some time."

After Zachary had ordered another beer and taken it off to his room, Carter headed to the nearby Belmopan hospital. His

107

gunshot wound in the shoulder needed looking at and there was yet another angle he wanted to check out.

Within fifteen minutes of his arrival at the hospital, he was in a clean consultation room, stretched out on a table as a registered nurse, a stately dark Belizian, removed the old bandage and began to ask Carter questions about allergies to various antiseptic and antibiotic substances. Her plastic name badge said she was Rose Cole.

"Fortunately for me, no allergies," Carter said.

"If I be any judge, you be very fortunate because it sure looks like you get shot at a lot." Rose Cole began to swab on an antiseptic cream, her strong fingers tracing the extent of Dr. Hakluyt's suturing. "It also look like you heal pretty good too. This one not going to leave a big scar."

Carter laughed. Scars were the least of his problems. They were his campaign badges. "Do you treat many gunshot wounds here?"

Rose Cole reflected for a moment. "We see more than we ought. What peoples about here got to shoot at each other for?"

"Is there some local feud?"

She chuckled. "Only feuds we be having is when some man don't marry that gal he be sleeping with for two, three years, and they have a few kids. Then her family be offended and there be threats back and forth about what happen if there be no ceremony and all. Stuff like that. But they too smart to go round settling things with guns. They use a witch."

"Do you believe in witches, Rose?"

"Well, we got two, maybe three gifted witches in the area, maybe one or two men who know their way around. So what happen, the offended gal's family, they pay a witch to make a spell that work so good, the man"—she gave a healthy chuckle—"the man can't have no truck with no other woman. He might just as well give up all thought of a sex life unless he marry that gal he start out with."

"So your feuds are fought with witches and spells?"

"That's the way with us," Rose Cole said. "We may not be high-tech, but a lot of us be happy."

At her direction, Carter sat. "I be removing these sutures now. They done their work and now you ready to mend on your own." She was an attractive woman, perhaps in her early thirties. Beginning to work on Carter, she watched him with an interest that went beyond the merely professional.

As she bandaged and taped, Carter pursued his line of questioning. "If the people around here are so peaceful, what accounts for the bullet wounds you've been seeing?"

"What I think, Mr. Carter, is dat they be lots of men like you hereabouts. They be playing soldier, and some of them just be plain silly or can't hit nothing."

"Where is all this taking place? Do you know?"

The nurse applied a final strip of adhesive. "I do it nice and tight, just like you say, so you can shower and bathe to suit you."

"You're not answering my question," Carter persisted.

She sighed and faced him, vexed. "You be a fine man, Mr. Carter. I can see how the ladies would be taken with you. But you sure do push." She handed him his shirt. "I see so many men with guns in the last ten years, how the hell do I know where they come or go? Some of them sweet-looking boys, trying to make a name for themselves. Some of them as mean and macho as you could want, and a lot of 'em like you, they seem easygoing enough if you don't push 'em, but plenty professional on the inside."

"Just one more thing," Carter said.

She smiled directly at him. "They be only one more thing you could give me any interest in."

The Killmaster met her gaze and smiled. "What can you tell me about that Center for the Arts?"

She humphed. "I should know you come here to get fixed up and go play soldier yourself instead of being interested in playing a more fun game, the basic boy-girl stuff," she said dryly. "That arts center, they be there five or six years. Before that, the buildings they be empty for maybe three or four years. Long enough for the jungle to start growing back in on it. Some peoples from the Bahamas and Mexico, they run a kind of resort where people come, eat silly little diet meals, and gamble. When that arts center start up, you hear all kinds of stories. I myself was called out there to help in some surgery. Surprising what an operating room they had."

Carter started to feel the excitement of a possible connection. "What kind of surgery?"

"I think they be calling it blunt trauma. That the way it

seem to me. Some man, his face be moved around quite a bit, they want to make sure he look all right, I guess. We work and work on him."

"Do you happen to recall the name of the doctor who did the surgery?"

Rose Cole smiled. "He be a strange man they all call Dr. Smith. Now, I may be a small-town gal, Mr. Carter, what you might call a hick. But I seen enough movies, read enough things. When a man from America call himself Smith, that mean his real name ain't none of your business."

Carter thanked Rose Cole. She'd had more information for him than he'd really expected. It had been a good break that she'd been on duty, and the results were beginning to make him eager to get moving. At the desk he was given a hefty but fair bill, which he paid, then he drove back to the inn. He was given a small, clean room next to Zachary. It seemed to him like a monk's cell in a monastery. The walls had been freshly whitewashed. The bed was a cot made of reject mahogany saplings and substantially laced with tanned leather strips.

As he ran a security check, Carter discovered that someone had been in the room during his absence. His bag wasn't squared with the edge of the bed as he'd left it. The drawer to the small writing desk had been closed flush against the frame, and Carter had deliberately left it ajar about a quarter of an inch. The pile of towels in the closet had been searched —and replaced with the manufacturer's label showing as opposed to the way Carter had left things.

He spent the next half hour checking for booby traps—innocent things that might be fatal for the unwary. At length he discovered that nothing had been rigged. Someone had merely wanted to check on him. Or perhaps someone had wanted Carter to know he was under surveillance.

Sinking into a soft but lumpy mattress, Carter felt frustrated, impatient. This entire business with LT reminded him of blood spreading in shark-filled waters. The renegade Prentiss starts the whole thing by a big discovery. Maybe he'd tumbled onto some of the Lex Talionis planning meetings. Then Cardenas, the Grinning Gaucho, gets into the picture. Possibly out of boredom with his laundered life in Phoenix. Possibly he sees a way to get back into a life-style that was more exciting. And now this business with Piet Bezeidenhout.

A man who has power, prestige, and enough security to satisfy the ordinary wealthy individual. But Bezeidenhout maybe has a bigger dream, one that takes him into power and influence on a global scale, and so what if he has to burn his former employers?

The difficult thing to piece into the puzzle now was Samadhi and his place in things.

Well, the hell with it. Carter was on the trail and he promised himself that tomorrow he'd be closer.

Nick Carter awakened to the sound of a distant rumble. He listened, Wilhelmina in his hand. He got up and moved out to the front porch. In the distance he saw headlights. A lot of headlights, moving in the night. A moment later Zachary appeared, rubbing sleep from his eyes. "I figure they truck in a lot of supplies around here, but that's more than a lot of supplies. That sounds like troop transports," he said. "A big convoy."

"Sure sounds like it," Carter agreed.

The rumbling continued, and in a few moments Carter returned to his room and began dressing. He fit Pierre into place carefully, strapped on the chamois sheath for Hugo, and holstered Wilhelmina under his left armpit. He took an extra clip and shoved it in his jacket.

Minutes later the two were in Carter's rental car, heading out toward the main highway, following the distant convoy on the road heading south.

They'd driven less than two miles when another vehicle, a restored World War II Jeep painted in jungle camouflage, loomed before them, its parking lights suddenly coming on. The Jeep was parked squarely in the middle of the road.

Carter had to jam on the brakes to avoid a collision.

One man in khakis and carrying an AK-47 at port arms shouted at them to turn around and go back. He pointedly shouted in English, Spanish, and French. Because of the man's ease with languages, Carter wondered if it were Unkefer, but there was no getting close enough to tell. Another man, his handgun holstered on his hip, made exaggerated movements that were impossible to misjudge. They were to turn around right now. No delay. No room for discussion.

"What do you think?" Zachary asked.

"I think we'll get a warning blast in another moment," Carter replied, shifting their Toyota into reverse. "And if we even look like we'd try to go around them, it won't be a warning anymore."

The shouted order to go back was repeated, followed immediately by a warning blast from the automatic weapon.

Carter spun the car around and headed slowly back toward Belmopan. They were followed for about a mile when the lights on the vehicle behind them went out.

"Old trick," Carter said. "They could still be in back of us or they could have pulled off and returned to the convoy. In either case, I think this is as far as we go tonight."

"Where do you suppose that convoy was headed?" Zachary asked. "I've checked with my people and we're sure not sponsoring anything around here."

"I'm not sure what this is yet," Carter said. "That was heavy equipment and we're close enough to Guatemala and Honduras to suspect possible *contra* activity, but I'm betting on Lex Talionis."

Nick Carter and Sam Zachary were up early the next morning, dressed in casual clothing and ready for the run out to the Belize Center for the Arts. They were going to play the role of intellectuals, and do some rubbernecking at the poetry festival.

Zachary ordered a breakfast of fried bananas, black beans, fish, and fruit. Carter had other things on his mind; he was eager to get going. He decided to take advantage of the microwave relay station. He left the room, found an isolated phone booth, and called David Hawk.

"Where the hell are you, N3?" The crusty director of AXE fired up a cigar. "We've got to see some results. The LT have been at it again. They've made a big score. They've taken three Japanese investment bankers."

"You're sure it's LT?"

"Damn sure," Hawk rasped. "They're taking credit for it, the bastards. They've already described things the bankers were wearing."

"Shit," Carter muttered. "I was just starting to think I had a line on how this worked. What kind of leverage could they get with Japanese investment bankers?"

"Try this, Nick. Money. A huge ransom."

"Of course," Nick Carter said. "Operating capital. The ransom is for operating capital."

"Find them, Nick. And soon."

The road to the arts center was well marked with more of the same hand-painted signs, the grading and paving different from the state roads. "They must build and maintain their own roads," Zachary said.

As they approached the center, they stopped at the point where they had been confronted the previous night. There were a few tread marks remaining in the surface dust of the roadbed, but scant other clues. They saw footprints, large enough to be a man's, probably wearing boots.

"Not one shell casing in sight," Zachary observed. "When we left, they probably combed the area and picked up the shell casings they fired at us."

"Either that," Carter suggested, "or the locals have the equivalent of a great lost golf ball business. They collect the casings and know where to sell them back."

He got out his notepad and sketched the patterns of the two distinctive tire-tread markings. One was a thick crosshatch, the other a large diamond pattern. Neither was notably unique. Carter looked at the footprints as well, finding one good set that had a new pair of Cat's Paw heels. Judging the size against his own foot, the Killmaster estimated the wearer of these boots was a size twelve, a beefy individual or one who carried a good deal of equipment.

Driving on, they began to notice a difference in the mountainous terrain. On either side of the road were broad savannas, lined by stands of trees in the distance. A semblance of landscaping began to appear, evidenced by symmetrical clumpings of bushes and arrays of wildflowers. A large stucco arch spanned the road, timeworn and cracked, but notably kept in some state of repair. In flowery letters was the logo for the Belize Center for the Arts. A cardboard sign welcomed all to the Spring Festival of the Arts.

As they continued, they saw a pond with a number of birds

and fountains. Soon the road broadened into a one-way drive circumnavigating a large bed of flowers and tropical plants. Now buildings began to appear, small, ornate outbuildings and then a larger two-story construction with covered porches. Most of the buildings were made of plaster and adobe slapped on heavily over lath. The large, two-story building had been put together by seasoned professionals. The buildings appeared completely out of place, in some state of shabbiness but still rather elegant and ornate, with designs at the tips and bottoms of decorative pillars. A freehand sign directed those who wanted the campgrounds to the rear, adding that there were electricity and water hookups.

Carter remembered what Rose Cole had told him about the place having once been a large gaming casino and fat farm. Now it was a center for performing and visual arts. Or was it?

Another sign directed them to a parking area, where yet another sign carried the designation REGISTRATION. The obvious place to go for that purpose was a smaller building with a Quonset hut roof and an identification plaque describing it as the administration area.

"Looks like a campus," Zachary said. "Feels like a campus."

The two men parked and walked toward the administration building, noting a steady hum of generators. A scattering of young men and women, looking much like students, moved in apparent leisurely purpose.

Five minutes later, for ten dollars American, Carter and Zachary were welcomed by some enthusiastic young men and women, signed up for the arts festival, and directed to another building, student housing, for their accommodations.

"You're in luck," a stout young woman with a New York accent said. "I have two single-room accommodations left."

Carter and Zachary were parted from more money and sold a meal ticket that entitled them to use the cafeteria. The young woman gave them a photocopied map of the center, marking the cafeteria, bookstore, and gift shop, where they could buy the distinctive Belize Center for the Arts sweatshirt or T-shirt. They were told that an orientation tour was under way in the central courtyard, and they could join it if they wished.

Zachary spoke under his breath to Carter. "Looks like

we're going to learn more about the Center for the Arts than we ever wanted to know, but we've got to check the place out."

As they headed toward the courtyard, they noticed a group of young men and women congregated in a group and Carter heard a distinctive voice with a touch of ethnic Pennsylvania in it. "There was a famous school in the U.S. in the forties," James Rogan said. "It was very famous because it produced a group of men and women who became the mainstream of poetry, writing, and teaching in this country for a long time. It was called Black Mountain. Our library has a lot of the work done by the Black Mountain people. I've consciously tried to model this place after Black Mountain. Hey, we're really going for a worldwide reputation here. We can be as good as we want to be."

Rogan, clad in a black turtleneck sweater and denims, made a broad, sweeping gesture to impress the group as a piercing whistle came from beyond the large complex of buildings.

Another whistle sounded almost immediately.

Carter and Zachary responded reflexively. The Killmaster dived for the first available cover and ducked into a protective crouch. Zachary darted behind a large pillar and tucked his head down against his shoulder. Both men had their mouths open as protection against what they knew was coming.

James Rogan and the group of students in the orientation group watched them, slack-jawed.

Soon, two heavy blasts rocked the area within seconds of one another. The first blast sounded like a huge kettledrum being struck. When the second blast came, it rattled windows and actually caused a number of them to shatter.

Although the explosions came from a distance, Rogan and a number of the students were stunned by them. Some were sprayed with a sooty debris. All felt a pain from the impact, and some rubbed at their ears, trying to get the whistling sensation to stop.

Carter and Zachary moved quickly from the cover they'd taken. A number of young people in the orientation group had begun to respond with screams and expressions of surprise and fear. One woman sat on the lawn and began to giggle uncontrollably. A young blond man in a preppy-looking shirt, chinos, and Topsiders looked dazed as blood began to trickle from his nose. "What's happened to me?" he said.

Recovering his balance, Rogan looked at Carter and Zachary. "What the hell's going on here?" he said. "Who are you guys?"

# FOURTEEN

James Rogan looked accusingly at Carter and Zachary. "You two, you ducked. *Before* the explosions, you both ducked. That was no accident, it was instinctive. You both ducked and protected yourselves."

"We've had experience in demolition," Zachary said blandly.

People were running in all directions, including two people with clipboards who wanted Rogan's attention.

"I'm not forgetting this," he said. "There's something going on here that I don't get. I've got to see what happened and what the damage was, but I want to talk to both of you."

"Let us come and help," Carter volunteered.

"Never mind that," the portly poet said. "We'll take care of our own stuff. If you guys are going to stick around for the festival, I'd appreciate it if you confined yourself to the buildings clearly marked on the map you were given. Is that understood?"

"I don't think you've got any problems with combustion," Carter said, sniffing the air. "Those were probably some kind of pipe bomb."

The words had a shattering effect on Rogan. "Pipe bombs? Why? Who would do such a thing here when we're trying to have a festival?"

"That's the sound of it," Carter said. "Someone was trying to knock out one of your systems or throw a scare at you. What's the source of your water?"

"What do you want to know that for?" Rogan asked, growing defensive.

"Someone might have wanted to knock out your water. Or

117

maybe your electricity. You obviously have a generator system."

"We've never had any trouble like this before. You guys, you stick around. I want to talk to you." Rogan asked an anxious middle-aged man with a bushy mustache to show him where it had happened. The man touched Rogan's sleeve and began speaking in a whisper. Rogan nodded nervously and let the mustached man lead the way toward the direction of the explosion.

As a well-organized group of students began moving around, checking for damage and injuries, Zachary smiled broadly at Carter. "You sure put the pressure on him."

"I think that's the only way we're going to find out anything."

"Do you," the CIA man asked, "suspect the same thing I do as the source of the bombs?"

Carter started off in the direction James Rogan had taken. "I tend to suspect Abdul Samadhi is behind it, yes," he said.

Ignoring Rogan's instructions, the two men began walking toward the point of the explosion.

A number of students and older people, Belizians from the look of them, stood around trying to restore order.

"Hey, you two. You're not allowed beyond this point," a young woman said as Zachary and Carter continued on their way.

"It's all right," Carter said. "Jim Rogan trusts our expertise with explosions."

"I thought I heard him tell you two to keep back," a familiar voice said. "We've got to clean this up on our own if we're going to save the festival."

Wearing jeans, sandals, and a Center for the Arts sweatshirt was Margo Huerta. She smiled mischievously at both men, and they both understood immediately that she wanted them not to let on that they knew one another. "We try to do everything Jim asks us," she said in an authoritarian voice. "This is a very democratic place, but we've got to have some rules. You understand?"

They got the break they were looking for when the young man with the bloody nose wandered by, seemingly disoriented. He sat on the edge of a neatly manicured lawn.

"He needs help," Carter said. "We've got to get him to the

dispensary." He put enough urgency in his voice that Margo Huerta understood his intent.

"I guess that can't harm anything." She pointed to a nearby building. "Around the corner from there and about a hundred yards to your right. There's a sign that says *Enfermería*."

Carter and Zachary lifted the young man under his elbows and got him to his feet. "Just a little woozy," he said. "I'm okay."

"Sorry," Carter told him with a covert wink at Zachary. "You're more than a little woozy. You've got some bone gristle showing."

"Oh, good Lord," the young man moaned.

"If we can get a doctor on it right away," Zachary said, "then there won't be any permanent damage."

By the time they reached the infirmary, the young man was in an agitated state, causing the attending nurse to respond with more than usual attention.

"You've got to get a doctor to look at this right away," Carter said. "This could be real trouble."

"We don't have a doctor in attendance except for emergencies," the nurse said. "And this looks straightforward enough. I'm sure I can handle it."

Zachary was at her, bullying, asking if she'd be willing to take the responsiblity for whatever happened to the young man. "I should think you'd want to make sure there was nothing wrong by getting a solid opinion."

The nurse caved in under the pressure. She sighed and got the young man to lie on an examining table. From her store of emergency treatment goods, she produced a chemical cold pack, which she twisted into activity. "Put this on your nose and try to relax."

The young man looked at her nervously. "Please hurry. I think I'm having trouble breathing."

"It's okay," Zachary said. "We'll stay with you."

Zachary kept up a continuous patter while the nurse was gone, keeping the young man's attention while Carter looked around, doing a quick study of the infirmary.

There were the usual boxes of sterile dressings, adhesive tapes, and Ace bandages. On one shelf, Carter found some neatly folded materials for slings and one or two braces for wrists and ankles; the Center for the Arts apparently had a program of athletics. Carter also found a great deal of topical anesthetics, sterile swabs, and the like.

Sophisticated equipment was at an absolute minimum; there were no drugs to speak of, but there were large containers of Lomotil pills, the drug of choice for the omnipresent cases of *turista*. It was by no means a remarkable dispensary, thoughtfully stocked but not equipped for anything out of the ordinary.

There was a container of materials next to a large sterilizer that bore a brass presentation plate inscribed *A Gift from the Kit Tremayne Living Memorial.* Carter poked about and found one or two scalpels and some tweezers and scissors.

The Killmaster had completed his survey of the room well before the nurse came back, followed by a man in a white smock, smoking a ropy-looking Toscani cigar, one of the types that David Hawk seemed to have going at all hours of the day or night.

The man was short, about the size and musculature of a jockey. He wore aviator-style glasses and moved with an exaggerated roll on Gucci loafers. He scarcely acknowledged Carter and Zachary's presence as he came in.

"What have we got here?"

As the doctor entered the room, the young man propped himself up on his elbows and removed the ice pack from his nose.

From a distance of ten feet the man in the smock scowled. "What the hell is this? What's your name?"

"Gug-Gonder, sir," the young man stuttered. "Bub-Bud Gonder."

The nurse became distraught. "I'm sorry, Doctor. I really was led to believe—"

The doctor ignored her. To the young man, he said, "Who did that to you?"

Bewildered, the young man said, "Sir?"

"Who did that butchery on your face?"

"There was an explosion—" the young man began.

"Screw the explosion! That was nothing so far as you're concerned. Someone did a nose job on you when you were a kid, right?"

Uncertainly, the young man nodded.

"Butcher!" the man in the smock said. "Whoever it was, he really butchered you, Gonder."

The doctor was leaning over the examination table, tracing his fingertips over the young man's nose, snapping instructions for the nurse to get him some sterile wipes.

Within five minutes, the doctor had the young man's face daubed clean, then he reached into his smock and extracted an examining light which he shone into the patient's nostrils. "Oakland," the doctor said. "Right?"

"Sir?"

"You're from Oakland, aren't you? Lake Merritt?"

"We-we lived there when I was younger."

"I thought so." The Doctor projected triumph. "Lawrence, right? Ronald Albert Lawrence of Oakland. That was the man who did this to your nose. Don't try to protect him, I can tell that butcher's work."

Within a short while, the diminutive doctor had the young man up and moving around. "You'd better come with me. I want to look into this at some greater length."

"I don't understand, sir," the young man said.

"Never mind," the doctor said, leading him out into the bright noon sun. "You just come with me, Gonder. I'll take care of everything." He draped a fatherly arm over the young man's shoulder and ushered him out the door. In leaving, he did not make eye contact with Carter or Zachary; he scarcely acknowledged the presence of the nurse.

"Come on," Carter said, leaving the infirmary and heading for the large grassy commons where students and participants were carrying on conversations, playing chess, or conducting small study groups. A griddle produced a steady stream of hamburgers on buns unlike anything Carter had ever seen, made from corn flour and a gritty substance Carter guessed was ground, dried hominy. Whatever the ingredients, the results were excellent, especially when doused with a tangy salsa made of tomatoes, green chiles, onions, and tomatillos.

"You know who that little guy is, don't you?" Zachary asked.

"Yeah. I didn't want to call him on it or spook him," Carter said, "but I'll give you odds that we just saw Dr. Charles Smith, an eccentric but gifted cosmetic surgeon."

Zachary said, "What's the scoop?"

Carter paused for a swallow of coffee. "The fact that he's here at all is the biggest break I've had in some time." He set the scenario for Zachary. "I hated to use that kid the way we did, but I know now that we're on the right track. We've got to find a way to nose around here on our own. If Smith is on the premises, there's every likelihood that he has his own operating room somewhere in the neighborhood." Carter smiled. "Things are starting to fall in place after all, my friend."

"You're thinking Smith did the reconstruct on that guy, Cardenas? The one who died at Covington?"

"Exactly," Carter said. "The Grinning Gaucho. The one you or your people were supposed to have heisted to prevent an autopsy. It makes sense now. Why would someone want an autopsy prevented?"

Zachary snapped his fingers. "To prevent the discovery of a Charles Smith reconstruction job."

"That's it," Carter said, standing. "I've got to make a phone call. I can see I let a potentially valuable piece of evidence get through the cracks."

"Any hints?" Zachary said.

"The Grinning Gaucho himself," the Killmaster said as he moved out onto the patio adjacent to the cantina.

Because of the excitement related to the bombing, Carter had to wait a half hour before he got to one of the most private of the pay phones.

David Hawk answered on the first ring.

"I need information," Carter said. "The only major metropolitan area near Covington, Kentucky, is across the river in Cincinnati. I need to know if there were any incidents of blunt trauma corpses being found there on or about the date of the Grinning Gaucho's death. Not just any old blunt force corpses. The one I'm looking for would significantly match Cardenas in weight, height, configurations."

"In other words, Nick, you think someone may have mutilated the body and dumped it to hide a cosmetic surgery job on Cardenas."

"I'd say it's ninety percent."

"What's next on your agenda?"

"Probably," Nick Carter said, knowing in advance the kind

of sputtering and fuming reaction it would produce, "I'll be going to a poetry reading."

The rooms assigned Carter and Zachary were located in a two-story arcade across a large patio from the dormitories. There were thoughtfully scattered chairs and tables in the patio, many of which were covered with the so-called little or literary magazines published by small groups and schools. The rooms of both men were on the ground floor. About ten feet wide and perhaps fifteen feet long, they held a minimum of furnishings: an institutional single bed, a modest desk and chair, and a larger, padded chair. In a small alcove was a vanity next to a sink. Each room had self-contained plumbing.

Carter put in an obligatory few minutes running a security check. So far as he could tell, no one had been in his room with the exception of a maid. His sensors picked up no recording or photographing devices.

Then, just as Zachary knocked on his door, he saw something he was intended to see.

"Come in, Sam."

The CIA man entered, clutching a sheet of paper. He saw Carter's pillow. "I see you got one too."

"Was yours on the bed?"

Zachary. "Right on the fluffed pillow." He noted they were both written by the same hand. A large circle with the letters *LT*. "Somehow I don't think this Lex Talionis logo has anything to do with Abdul Samadhi," the CIA operative said.

"Neither do I," Carter said.

"But someone is clearly warning us off."

Carter offered Zachary one of his cigarettes. "I don't think it has to be that way." He paused, savoring a developing thought. "I'm beginning to come up with its being something entirely different."

Sam Zachary smoked for a moment, reflecting. He snapped his fingers. "Margo Huerta!"

"Possible," Carter said, "but that doesn't make too much sense to me."

"Okay, then," Zachary said, "you're thinking way ahead of me. Tell me what you're working on."

"My line of logic goes like this: there's someone who knows what we're doing here and who we are. That person wants us to know how close we are to the big stuff."

"Then our next move is to get ourselves some space and check these grounds out in as much detail as we can."

"That's not going to be easy," Carter said. "We've got the problem of Rogan not trusting us. But let's go."

They agreed on different directions.

Carter set off toward a large ornate pink building that looked like an auditorium.

Zachary took off toward the administration building.

Each carried notebooks and made no move to look furtive.

Carter was stopped just beyond the big pink building. A man with a brown beret, rolled-up sleeves, and thick-soled shoes said, "You can't go there. Please stick to the areas located on your map." Conspicuous on his hip was a webbed belt, a leather holster, and something that was big enough to be a .45.

"What's over there?" Carter asked innocently.

"Buildings from the old days. Closed down now. In a year, maybe two, they'll be dormatories."

"Is there a library around here?"

The man nodded. "Building C-two on your map."

"Why do you need a gun?"

"Snakes," the man said.

Carter smiled at him. "You hit many snakes with that forty-five?"

"There are large areas where the public is welcomed," the man said. It was a speech he'd had to memorize to get the job. "We encourage outings and do our best to provide for your safety."

"Suppose I was willing to take the risk of going over there?"

"It's not an option, sir," the guard said.

Carter took off on a tack beyond the pink building, bringing him on a forty-five-degree path beyond the commons and cafeteria building. He left a wide gravel path and strolled leisurely across a grassy knoll and had got nearly a quarter of a mile before he heard a sharp voice commanding him to stop.

The guard this time was a woman who wore a short blue canvas skirt, ankle-high aerobic shoes, and a chambray work shirt like Carter's. She was even better armed than the last guard. Slung over her shoulder was a Kalashnikov. "Sorry, sir, my instructions are to keep you to the paths and areas marked approved on the map you were issued when you came in."

"You know how to use that thing?" Carter nodded his head at the Kalashnikov.

"That's affirmative, sir. I have three weeks training a year with it."

"Use it for the snakes, right?"

She shook her head. "Hardly any snakes here, sir. You may have noticed a large cat population. Even if there were snakes, the cats would get to them quickly."

"What do you need that heavy artillery for?"

"Uh, sir, this is part of the Center for the Arts security forces."

Carter shook his head. "You haven't answered my question. What are you protecting us from? Bandits? *Contras?*"

"Sorry, sir, I walk my rounds and follow my instructions. If you have questions about the center's security, you're free to take them up with the director."

Carter took off in yet another direction, with the same results. He was sent back by an armed guard.

Carter outlasted Zachary by ten minutes. The CIA man had been stopped by armed persons who'd sent him back to the areas indicated on the map.

They were forced to join an orientation and discussion group in which Jim Rogan gave a lengthy discourse on the explosions and their significance.

"These guys here," he said, pointing to Carter and Zachary, "said the explosions were probably pipe bombs and as nearly as we can tell, they were right. There did not appear to be any specific target. None of our buildings or utilities were damaged. There were some broken windows and debris, but that's the extent." He looked at them with fatherly concern. "I've provided some security forces to check things out and to make sure you're all okay."

While Rogan spoke, justifying his armed guards, Carter realized it was going to make investigating the surroundings that much more difficult.

"Why would anyone want to set off a bomb here?" an incredulous and serious young woman with a straw hat said.

"We're working on it," Jim Rogan said. "But don't worry, we'll keep our guard up. And we won't let it interfere with our festival. We'll have our workshops and our readings. Remember, wherever you go, you'll be safe. But just to make sure, I ask that you don't stray beyond the marked buildings on the map that came with your registration packet."

"There's no way for us to get out tonight for a look around," the Killmaster said. "He'll have someone posted to watch us. If we don't even try, and participate in some of the other activities, it will get his guard down."

Zachary groaned. "This is not going to be easy stuff to take."

Carter gave him an encouraging clap on the shoulder. "Just think of it all being for a good cause. We can get free tomorrow night and find out what the hell's at the other side of these grounds."

The evening passed with agonizing slowness. A tall woman in her early thirties, speaking with a working-class English accent, appeared to be taken with Zachary and tried to sit near him and engage the CIA man in conversation.

At the dinner hour, they were served some black beans and rice and macaroni and cheese. Although the cheese was tangy enough, Zachary balked. "Thank goodness for my war chest in my room." In desperation, he went to the cantina and found a few candy bars, and when that didn't do the trick, he bribed one of the Belezian cafeteria workers, who produced a roast pork sandwich with fresh lettuce and a piquant salsa, which he shared with Carter.

Discussion groups were formed and Carter made efforts to engage Rogan with questions that were related to the agenda of poetry. "Would you please," he said, "give us your theory about the need for relevant imagery?"

The portly director was delighted with the question and spent a half hour expounding on it. Questions and open discussion lasted yet another hour. The Englishwoman, looking at Zachary as she spoke, took issue with Rogan, no doubt trying to impress Zachary.

Carter looked at his watch. It was nearly ten o'clock. Not a bad night's work, considering how boring it was.

Rogan read some more of his work and the work of others he'd translated from various languages.

Zachary was soon inspired with a question of his own. "Would you please discuss in some detail the obligations of a translator to the integrity of the original work?"

The Englishwoman beamed with satisfaction, as though it had been the very thing she'd come to hear about. "Here, here," she said, applauding faintly.

Her response was not lost on Rogan, who looked at his watch and sighed thoughtfully. "Maybe we can get at that tomorrow, in the morning session," he said with a hopeful nod.

Zachary was right there with the pressure. "Hey, I thought we came here to be serious and work. Isn't that what you said? I read that the discussions at Black Mountain went on all night when the students and teachers began really communicating."

Rogan looked at him for a moment, trying to make up his mind.

The Englishwoman spoke out in outrage. "You were the one who said this was to be a working session."

At length Rogan smiled. "Okay," he relented. "I can see you people are serious. I can see what this all means to you."

"Damned right," Zachary said as Rogan began, once again, to expound on a subject that was dear to his heart.

The session broke up at eleven-thirty with Carter, Zachary, and an elderly man who wore a bow tie trying to prolong things, asking still more questions.

Rogan held up his pudgy hands and said, "I really appreciate all this energy. I've got an assignment to give you, and you can be working on it tonight and we'll look at the results tomorrow."

While the students took notes, Rogan assigned a topic for them to write about.

"Does that sound like makework to you?" Zachary whispered.

Carter shook his head. "I think he's serious. I don't think he's trying to get away for any reason other than he's tired."

As they headed to their rooms, the Englishwoman asked Zachary if he'd like to come to her room for a nightcap. She very nearly blushed when she said, "I have a little flask of cognac."

Zachary was tempted by the prospect of the cognac, but he politely refused.

"I think we've done ourselves some good," Carter said. "In

the meantime, don't even go out to have a smoke once you've turned in. Tomorrow night we'll take advantage of the fact that we have ground-floor rooms with large enough windows to crawl out of."

"Gotcha," the CIA man said. "But it's going to be a bitch getting through the day."

"Think of it as being like stakeout duty," Carter suggested.

"I'll take stakeout to this crap any old time." Zachary opened his door, waved, and disappeared inside.

Carter walked to his room.

He inserted the key in the ancient latch and let himself in.

The light switch brought no response. The Killmaster flattened himself against the wall, a twitch of his forearm muscle bringing Hugo instantly into his palm.

Someone was in the room with him.

The Killmaster waited for his eyes to grow accustomed to the dark.

# FIFTEEN

Carter could hear the shallow breathing of someone who was excited, someone trying to control his own breathing.

He placed his visitor near the bed. He thought about throwing Hugo at the direction of the breathing, estimating his chances for a hit.

The woman's voice spoke in a soft whisper. "Don't you think after all this time I should find my way to your bed, Nick Carter?"

"You almost bought yourself some extra ventilation, Margo," Carter told her. "That was a foolish thing to do to achieve a dramatic effect."

"You come here," she said in the darkness, "and I'll show you everything you need to know about dramatic effects."

Carter swore under his breath and replaced Hugo in his chamois sheath. "Could anyone have seen you come in here?"

She sniffed disdainfully. "See how you begin to patronize me instead of accepting the gift that is yours? I was very careful. I finished my chores sometime back. No one is expecting me, and no one is keeping track of me as they are you."

"You know that for a fact?"

"I heard Rogan tell two of his staff to watch you and Zachary tonight and to report"—she chuckled—"to report any movements."

"What's so funny?"

"You are about to make some very interesting movements. Come sit next to me, Carter. It is time for us to meet our destiny."

129

"You wouldn't be one of those assigned to report my movements, would you, Margo?"

Carter could feel her anger flare in the darkness.

"You still don't trust me, do you," she said, her voice raised with indignation. "After everything we've been through, the risks I have taken? After I have provided you and your friends with vital leads, you still have your doubts about me?"

"I've been in this business for a long time," Carter said, "and I'll admit there's a good deal I do by the book, procedures proven to work. But there's also an instinct I've learned to trust, and something about you turns on my warning sirens."

She turned on the lamp on the nightstand. A small pool of light from a low-wattage bulb made it possible for Carter to now see clearly that she was in his bed, naked, her clothes neatly folded over a chair.

"So much for your warning sirens, Carter. This was to have been yours for the taking." She cupped her hands under her ample and shapely breasts, lifting suggestively.

Carter watched her without comment.

"All the hidden delights were to have been yours," she said, running her hands over her hips in an inviting, frank manner, her tongue flickering over her lips and moistening them. "There is unfinished business between us from before."

Naked, she was a beautiful and erotic sight, her body sleek, her dark hair pulled back so that the long curve of her neck was emphasized. Now her legs began to part suggestively.

"That was quite an interesting note you left earlier today on my bed," Carter said.

"What note? I left you no note, Carter. I have been here perhaps half an hour, but not before then."

Carter moved to the padded chair and sat, kicking off his loafers.

Margo Huerta swung her shapely legs over the side of the bed and began to approach him. Watching her, seeing her naked opulence, Carter was strangely unmoved. In a moment she sensed it and posed, hands on her hips. "What of all the chemistry between us before, Carter?" She seized upon an idea. "I know what it is," she said in triumph. "You still carry a torch for that little Mossad girl, don't you?"

Carter had not thought about Rachel Porat for some time, but now the mention of her name brought back the memory of their lovemaking in Phoenix, and the image of her trim, compact body was very much with him.

"You see?" Margo said. "I was right. I can see what the mention of her does to you."

"We have a problem," Carter said, "or maybe I'm the one with the problem. This room is being watched to see what if any my movements are. You'll surely be noticed if you leave now, so it looks as if I'm stuck sleeping on this chair and you take the bed."

Margo approached him and delivered a stinging slap to his cheek. He felt the heat of it spread slowly. "You are a beast, Carter, to treat me like this. I am not used to being treated this way by men."

Carter realized the slap was sincere. It again gave him pause that maybe he was wrong. "Unless you can figure a way to get out of here without being seen, it's the bed for you and the chair for me."

She whirled and jumped on the bed in a fury. Carter smiled and took the chair.

At two o'clock Margo propped herself up on her elbows. "Carter," she said, "are you asleep?"

"Yes," Carter said mechanically.

"You could still be here, with me. We could have the rest of the night together."

Carter realized that was probably true and wondered if he was wrong. Margo Huerta was an attractive woman; it would undoubtedly be a memorable experience to make love with her. Was he passing up a splendid opportunity for no real reason?

But again the internal warning sounded and Carter knew he would have to be governed by it; he would accept the consequences of his own instincts, silly or not. He had lived with those instincts for too long now.

"Close your eyes and try to get some sleep," he told her. "Thinking about it isn't going to make it any better. It'll only keep you awake."

In the darkness Margo hissed a Spanish word across the gap that separated them. *"Maricón!"*

Carter laughed quietly. "Now, Margo," he said, "you know that isn't true. Try to get some sleep."

*"Cochon!"*

"That's better," Carter said. "Pig is okay."

At four o'clock Margo called out again. "Carter," she said. "Can you hear me?"

"Go to sleep, Margo."

"First I want to tell you."

"Tell me what?"

"I really respect you, Carter. You're absolutely right. I wanted you just because we're in something frightening and I'm horny and I wanted to prove that I could make you care for me. It was you and my own fears I was really after. I apologize, *compadre*. Is it okay between us now?"

"It's okay, Margo. Go to sleep."

"Listen, Carter, let me take the chair for a while and you take the bed."

At five-thirty they began hearing sounds of life outside and by six o'clock there were the unmistakable smells of coffee and the aroma of frying bacon. Carter showered, shaved, got dressed, and headed for Zachary's room. If he were still being watched, that would give Margo a chance to get out of his room unnoticed.

The CIA agent offered Carter a cup of freshly brewed coffee that helped clear the mists in his head. Last night had not been easy. "You look a bit done in," Zachary said.

Carter noticed the same of Zachary.

The CIA man handed Carter an English muffin, toasted on a small gas stove from his war chest. "Marmalade or damson plum preserves?" Zachary said, causing Carter to marvel at his resourcefulness.

"The mountain would not come to Mohammed," he said, "and so Vanessa came to the mountain. She is a demure-looking lady, but she has some intriguing moves." Zachary pinched the bridge of his nose. "I have not had a cognac hangover for some time," he said with a wince. "Here, let me pour you some more coffee."

There were pads of paper on the small desk, and while they ate their breakfast, the two men went resolutely to work on the writing assignment Jim Rogan had given the night before. "We've got to get clear to do a thorough investigation," Carter recounted, "and if we play Rogan's game, we'll get the best opportunity to get free."

Groaning loudly from time to time, Zachary recalled some material from his college days and later reading. Carter worked on something he remembered from one of the Russian dissident writers. The two men finished another pot of Zachary's good Jamaican coffee while working on their assignments, then they went to the cafeteria and managed some bacon and eggs. Carter noticed the pay phone was free and moved to it to call David Hawk.

Even though it was apparently a standard pay phone, Carter thought it best to use precautions. This was going to be a sensitive conversation with no way to talk around things. "You'd better put this call on scramble," he advised. "Try range two."

From his wallet, Carter extracted a circuit board the size and approximate thickness of a credit card. Across the middle was a round green membrane the size of a half dollar. Carter held the card directly over the mouthpiece of the phone, then began to speak.

"What did Cincinnati say, sir?"

The crusty AXE director lit a cigar. "You hit the mark, Nick. Cincinnati was most cooperative and impressed. They report an unclaimed traumatic force corpse that appeared about three days after the Grinning Gaucho business in Covington. They'd been on the telex to a number of agencies. Really responsible people."

"How about the ID?"

"The corpse had been in the river for sometime," Hawk said. "That didn't leave much to work on. Significantly, the fingerprints had been eaten away and the face was battered beyond recognition. But the size, apparent weight, and general body characteristics are a good match with our man."

"How about a dental match to make certain?" Carter said.

"No longer possible, Nick. The corpse was kept for the required period of time, the usual notices sent out. It was sent to the medical school anatomy department. The soggy mortal remains of the Grinning Gaucho are probably quite spread out among a number of young men and women who are the future doctors of America."

He paused, took in some smoke, and exhaled with pleasure. "How's your poetry venture?"

Carter told him of the episode with the doctor. "I'm betting it's Charles Smith. You might check for me to see if we're dealing with a five-foot-five or five-foot-six male Caucasian, dark brown hair, weight about a hundred and ten or fifteen."

"Will do," Hawk said.

"Any news on those Japanese investment bankers taken as hostages by LT?"

Hawk sounded concerned. He told Carter of the pressure he'd been getting to develop some leads on the three men. "Believe it or not, that's having a direct effect on the market value of the dollar and on the stock market. You can imagine how that trickles down to me. And now it's landed in your lap." He took in smoke, then let it out with a sigh. "I'm almost tempted to pull you off what you're doing to have a look at all the evidentiary materials."

Carter's response cheered Hawk when he told him, "I believe we're going to find a connection between the kidnapped investment bankers and that so-called gas main explosion in Los Angeles. I think we're going to find all these activities tie in with LT." He told Hawk about the notes he and Zachary had received and about his belief that they were intended as clues. "I'll of course obey your instructions," Carter said, "but I urge you to consider that I'm in the right place now."

"Fine, fine," Hawk said, "but keep pushing." He reflected for a moment. "I can tell you for a fact, Nick, that the explosion in Los Angeles was a bomb. The gas main story was trumped up from the beginning."

"It may be a little late in the game to ask you this, but it was you who taught me the virtues of checking on everything."

Hawk blew out smoke.

"The CIA man, Sam Zachary. He claims he met you at a gathering hosted by you at your place."

"Quite right, Nick, it's always important to check. Yes, I've seen him two or three times socially. I frankly can't understand what he sees in that bunch at Langley. He isn't their sort at all. More of a loner. Good man. I did a stealth inquiry on him and discovered he hadn't cashed a paycheck in over a year. You'd think they wouldn't notice, the way they throw around their discretionary funds and all, but it played havoc with their payroll and they called him on the carpet."

Hawk smoked, began to chuckle. "His excuse was that he'd forgotten."

"You wouldn't have that trouble with me, sir," Carter said."

"This is highly confidential and is not to go beyond you. It seems Zachary is independently wealthy. He came from a middle-class family, but married into real money. He refused their help, worked at securities trading, and amassed a tidy fortune all on his own. The marriage failed, and even though his ex-wife's family can well afford his son's education, he regularly contributes a handsome stipend for the boy."

"One more personnel status check, please," Carter requested. "The individual is James Rogan." Carter told him what he knew, which Hawk took down, still chuckling to himself about the background on Sam Zachary.

Carter and Zachary had a last cup of coffee in the cafeteria and moved to join a group of students and Jim Rogan in a small but comfortable auditorium.

They handed their assignments to the chubby director who smiled, scanned them briefly, then looked at the two with admiration. "These guys," he said, "really entered into the spirit of things. They got their assignments done and in the process addressed significant ideas. I'm proud of you. Incidentally, they were the only two to complete their work so far. The rest of you get busy."

Finding a seat with Zachary, Carter whispered behind the back of his hand. "I hope that little exercise raises our credibility."

Rogan bounded up on the stage and took his place at a heavy plank table with microphones. Two men and two women sat on either side of Rogan, clearly the members of a panel discussion.

Zachary groaned, then whispered, "I can't believe we've got to sit through this until tonight."

They did have to sit through it, and both men plowed in. It was part of their job.

At the dinner break, Carter did a search on his room and

determined to his satisfaction that no one had been inside. Wandering past the cafeteria area, Carter decided to force the issue and see if he could determine if anyone was still watching him.

He headed to the points where he'd been stopped by the armed guards. They were not on duty. He pushed his incursions well beyond where he'd been told not to go. To double check, he blended into the scenery, doubled back, and waited to see if he were being allowed to go forth while still under surveillance.

To his satisfaction, the trail was clear.

He headed toward the building that looked like an athletic facility, entered, and began looking around. After about half an hour of looking, Carter found things as they'd been represented. There were piles of construction-grade lumber, some scaffolding, some bags of plaster. From what Carter could put together, this had once been a luxurious spa. Now it was destined to become a swimming pool and a few basketball and volleyball courts.

He left the building, deciding Jim Rogan had called off the watchdogs, whoever they were. That meant the stage was set for some reconnaissance.

He went to his room to shower, change his shirt, and prepare for the night ahead. The Killmaster knew he was coming closer to Lex Talionis all the time. Tonight would be important. At the slightest trace of a solid lead, he'd have to take the risk of blowing cover. He'd have to go in for the kill.

Zachary knocked, entered his room, and spoke in a guarded professional whisper.

"It's starting to hit the fan," he said, reaching for his wallet. "I called my contact. Do you use one of these scramblers?" He held up a small plastic card.

Carter nodded.

"Remember I told you my people got burned for a million?"

Carter nodded again.

"I got my call through and found out that Piet Bezeidenhout burned the South African diamond cartel for something like five million dollars and—get this—the cartel has put a contract out on him. They want him dead. They're willing to pay a million American for his corpse."

"That settles it," Carter said. "He's made his break and is probably the leader of LT. They want a lot of money for some big operations. The question now is what. What is the LT organization up to? And how much time do we have to stop them?"

# SIXTEEN

Carter and Zachary took the available maps of the Center for the Arts and divided them up in a grid system, each choosing a different area for their sweep. They would begin by ignoring more obvious areas located near the front of the campus and focus on the more remote areas on this side of Belmopan. They would use a standard military pattern to make sure they covered the most significant amount of area in the least amount of time.

Zachary had a liquid Swiss lensatic compass. Carter carried one of the newer Japanese infrareds with rechargeable battery.

Carter was quite sure that Margo would not come back to his room, but now they were faced with the likelihood that the Englishwoman, Vanessa, would hope to visit Zachary. Their decision was to put signs on their doors: *Busy writing. Please do not disturb*.

The lectures and workshops were over by eleven. A nearly full moon was up. The students were fidgety from sitting still all day, stimulated by some of the better speakers, and keyed up by some of the questions Carter and Zachary had asked to stave off their boredom. A number of them had invited Carter and Zachary to impromptu rap sessions, but when the two men spoke of wanting to work on their material, they were excused with admiration.

The Englishwoman made some broad hints to Zachary, who put her off lightly by telling her he'd come knocking later—if he had any energy left. "You are a very intense woman," he said, satisfying her immensely.

The light from the moon would cause trouble, but the two

had to draw a line and not make it too obvious by the way they dressed that they were on a stealth mission. "I'm not planning on being caught," Carter said, "but if we're seen, I think it important to be able to give a convincing story and say we were out for a walk and lost track of the time."

"No blackening on the face, in other words," Zachary said. "Nor black watch cap or turtleneck."

Zachary had an extra pair of jeans that Carter had to roll at the cuff. Carter wore black fitness shoes, and Zachary had a pair of dark blue Nikes that, unfortunately, had reflecting surfaces for night running. Zachary found some mud and daubed it in place.

The men checked weapons, infrared sighting devices, and mosquito repellant. They arranged a time and place where they should meet in their systematic sweep. With that, they taped the notes to their doors.

Easing open his back window and carefully lowering himself out, Carter checked to make sure he was not seen. The tropical air was balmy and fragrant. The Killmaster felt a surge of energy and excitement.

He moved within twenty yards of a group sitting in lawn chairs by the patio. Another few hundred yards along his path, there were the unmistakable sounds of a couple making love.

Checking his compass, he moved off at a brisk pace in a northeasterly direction, moving in the shadow of buildings whenever possible, switching to gravel or areas that would not show footprints. Gradually, sounds receded. No more portable tape decks or radios, no more ardent voices of arguing students.

By the time he judged he was a good distance from the main portion of the campus, he saw that the landscaping had been almost completely abandoned. The lawns were shaggy, overgrown. Tropical foliage grew in carefree abandon.

He reached his designated area and began his sweep, moving through the thick underbrush, hearing nothing now but the sounds of jungle animals, insects, and night birds. Mosquitoes dived at him, backing off when they became aware of his repellant.

Twice during the next hour Carter risked using his halide flashlight for traces of paths or installations. Increasing his pace, he moved impatiently into his next grid area, covering ground, seeing all he could, finding nothing of significance.

It was not until just before his scheduled meeting with Zachary at two o'clock that he came across the traces of a small encampment. Circling the area carefully to make sure no one was nearby, he came back and shone his flashlight on the traces of a cooking fire circled with heat-retaining lava rocks.

Someone had been careful enough—or bored enough—to have done an elaborate job with the rocks. Off to one side, Carter found freshly dug areas, and when he found a sturdy tree limb to poke at them, he found carefully buried cans and garbage. Further down from the cooking fire was a place where at least one person had slept and smoked.

Carter estimated he had about a mile to cover before his meeting with Zachary. Because of the discovery of the camp, he had to be careful. It could be nothing, perhaps just some adventurous students. Or it could be an advance guard.

When he reached the rendezvous area, Carter scanned with his infrared scope and would have been content to wait in silence for the CIA man except that his shoes dug into something in the terrain that felt uncharacteristic. Dropping to his haunches, he found several sets of tire tracks. He quickly reached for his sketch pad but realized he wouldn't have to. One was a crosshatch, the other a bold set of large diamonds. He'd seen them both before.

In the darkness, Carter cursed himself for not thinking to get a look at the treads of the large diesel bus he'd worked on for Unkefer. Playing his infrared scope over the area, he was surprised to discover several dozen spent .762 NATO rounds. The locals apparently weren't able to work this territory. Too much risk back here.

Carter gave the signal of a snapping twig, followed by another in quick succession.

No response.

He moved cautiously about the area, deciding to give Zachary another ten minutes before signaling again, but off to his left he could hear a steady movement now, something or someone moving through the jungle night.

Carter took cover behind the trunk of a particularly large tree, leaned on it to steady himself, and turned on his infrared scanning scope.

Through the lens screen he saw a man perhaps in his early

thirties wearing olive drabs and combat boots, and carrying an automatic rifle. Some twenty feet from him was Sam Zachary, poised and waiting with a small, deadly noose.

Carter watched in silence, knowing the patrol man was not aware of Zachary, that Zachary would neither attack nor kill unless it became necessary to prevent their discovery.

The patrolling man stopped, lit a cigarette, and propped himself against the side of a tree. From the acrid tang, Carter could tell the tobacco was a Delicado or one of the cheaper Mexican or Guatemalan brands. Carter would want to check it to see if it matched the butts by the camp he'd found earlier.

Like many cheap brands, the cigarette went fast. The man swigged at a bottle, probably some cactus brandy, shuddered from the enjoyment of it, wiped his mouth, and soon was on his way, moving off at about a forty-five-degree angle from Carter.

Waiting for his footfalls to vanish in the distance, Zachary stepped forward.

"Well?" Carter said.

"That was nothing," Zachary said. "I can show you a large group of them. Wanna see?"

"Mark the position, and we'll take a look the next time through. Tonight's our getting-oriented venture."

They walked in silence for nearly two miles on ground that was largely level, rose only slightly toward a forest draw, then abruptly fell away to a steep grade.

Zachary whispered something about prehistoric volcanic action. "Whatever it was," he said, "look what it set up for us." He and Carter removed their infrared scopes and peered down the draw.

Below them were three small buildings, made of adobe and the thick Belezian timbers, with thatched roofs. They were small but substantial, with a number of shuttered windows. Several vehicles were parked nearby: at least two Jeeps, a troop transport, and a six-by-four truck. There was a well-made fire pit much like the one Carter had seen earlier. A cheery fire smoldered in the night. The camp security was not great. One man sat sleeping, his head resting on his knees; another man read a comic book by the light of the fire.

"You've been pretty good with your educated guesses," Zachary said with admiration. "Now I've got a hunch of my own. There are about three guys down there who'd be very happy for some sushi right now—three investment banker types."

Carter was genuinely growing to enjoy Zachary. "That's no guess, Sam. You had some time and you were down there and you saw them firsthand."

"You got me," Zachary admitted. "That's just what I did. Those people are so relaxed and sure of themselves that we could go in and take the Japanese out of there right now."

Noting the time, Carter said, "It's worth the risk. We've got to try for it."

Carter set up the operation in segments.

He went down first, and took out the guard who was reading the comic book. He pushed heavily on the man's carotid artery, and when the guard had passed out, he trussed him with his belts.

The guard who'd been asleep came awake with the beginnings of a yell. Carter had to put Hugo to work, right through the throat. Bloody, but fast.

He gave Zachary the signal and the CIA man began taking all the vehicles out of commission except the Jeep that had the fullest tank.

Carter went through the weapons he'd taken from the guards, settled on two .45s, and put those in the Jeep. They'd be insurance for the investment bankers.

To Zachary he said, "See if you can do a quick sort and find a map that will get these guys out of here and back to Belize City."

The CIA man smiled. "Already on the driver's seat. What next?"

"I'm going to hit the house. Check to see if you can find any phone lines, alarm systems, or radio devices. Take care of them."

Checking Wilhelmina's action, Carter moved on the house. In the back room, two more guards were playing cards for American dollars, a combination of gin and draw poker.

They looked up at Carter with bewilderment. "I know it looks tacky, our playing cards, sir," one of them said. "But we've got the place well secured."

"Really," the other said.

"How wrong you are!" Carter leveled two blasts at them. Their card-playing days were over.

A tangy odor reached Carter and he realized what a break he'd had. There was someone else in the house, cooking a meal for the prisoners. Probably someone who knew Japanese cooking. That could have been trouble.

She was young and small, and looked to be in her early twenties. There were strong traces of the Orient in her delicate cheeks and brow. She was probably a mixture of Filipino and Japanese, with maybe a few other touches. She had the kitchen going with boiling water and things sizzling on a brazier. In a white smock that was a bit too small for her, she was quite an eyeful—enough to make any man stop and turn.

Carter hit the door fast and advanced on her, Wilhelmina in hand.

"No!" she cried. "Please! No!" She shook her head, trying to indicate she'd do nothing to raise an alarm.

She was frightened but made no move to go on the attack. There was a sudden weariness in her face. Men had seen her and wanted things. Her small, sharp breasts. Her tiny waist and graceful hips. A beautiful, poor woman, used to having no control over her one asset. Her almond eyes sought his, pleading for no violence.

"Take off your stockings," Carter directed.

She looked at him and began to whimper.

"It isn't what you think," he said softly. "I have to tie you."

She sat, removed her shoes, and began to cry. "Ah, God," she said, "it always happens this way."

Carter noticed that she wore a handwoven Indian sash around her waist. He motioned her to the floor, turned her on her stomach, drew her wrists together, and secured them with one stocking. Then he went to work on her ankles with the other. With the sash, he tied wrists and ankles together.

"I'm not making the knots tight," Carter said. "I can't take the chance that you'll follow or call out for help. I need time."

She was not going to be particularly comfortable, but she wasn't going to suffer.

He shredded a towel to make a gag. She began whimpering.

Before he could place the gag, Zachary signaled that the

outside was secure. "I'm going to circle the place just in case we missed anything," he said.

Carter nodded and hit the door, both hands on Wilhelmina.

The Japanese bankers were in a state of lethargy from their ordeal. At first they sprang to attention, caught by the sudden adrenaline, but as Carter went from door to door, room to room, protecting himself, looking for any other guards, they came to regard him as merely another crazy Westerner.

"Do any of you speak English?" he asked in Japanese.

They all nodded. They were in their forties, wearing the fine custom-tailored suits they'd had on at the time they'd been taken. Their experience made them jumpy, resigned.

"How often do the guards come to check?" Carter asked.

The only one of the three who did not wear glasses spoke. "The longest they leave us is two hours. They are nearly due. A girl nearby cooks for us."

Carter went into the next room, hefted the young woman, and brought her back inside. "Is she the one or is she a substitute?"

All three shook their heads. "She was the only one. She was good to us."

"Do any of you drive an automobile?"

One nodded.

"A Jeep. Four-wheel drive?"

There was a silence. The bankers looked at one another nervously. "Automatic. Chrysler Imperial."

Zachary knocked on the outside wall. "All clear at the moment."

Carter moved to the window. "They say we can expect some inspection at any time now. I think we've got to get them in the Jeep and get them going right now. You and I stick it out for the inspection team. Buy these guys as much time as possible."

"I'll do one more circle and meet you by the Jeep," Zachary said.

"There's just one problem," Carter said. "Only one of these guys drives and he can't handle a stick shift much less four-wheel drive."

"There's a shift diagram right over the lever," Zachary said. "He'll have to learn fast."

"I can drive four-wheel," the woman said timidly.

"You're sure?"

She nodded.

"That's it. This operation's blessed," Zachary said. He pounded the side of the building and was gone.

By now it was beginning to dawn on the Japanese that they were being rescued. "You are brave to do this."

"What did your captors tell you?" Carter said. He quickly began to untie the young woman.

"After we are brought here, we meet a stocky man—"

"—with short blond hair—"

"—yes, and he wears wire glasses. Afrikaner. Man named —"

"Bezeidenhout?" Carter prompted.

All three Japanese nodded.

"What did he tell you?"

"He said he had picked us carefully. That we were part of a big venture. Bigger than any multinational or offshore capital venture the world has ever known. We would bring him millions of Japanese yen."

"Ransom," Carter muttered to himself. "A big, big score." He looked intently at the nervous trio. "Okay, here's what I want you to do," Carter told the Japanese investment bankers, leading them outside toward the Jeep. He tugged the girl gently by the wrist, bringing her along. "There isn't much time, and you must obey my instructions carefully."

The bankers followed Carter to the Jeep, listening to him give directions to Belize City to their cook. Then he told them what they must do when they arrive. "You go to a hotel with a telephone. Call the Japanese embassy in Mexico City. Identify yourselves, and tell them what has happened to you and where you are. Don't open the door for anyone who can't convince you that you ought to. Do you understand that? You go only with your own people. Okay?"

"We are in your debt a thousand times."

"Once is enough," Carter said, sliding behind the wheel of the Jeep and firing the engine.

"How can we repay you?"

"Simple," Carter said. "There are bound to be police involved in this. They will ask you questions and show you maps. You are smart gentlemen and have traveled around the world, no doubt. I want you to promise that you will not bring them back here. You will not show them the way. You will forget where you were. That's the price, understood?"

"You want this place for yourself?" one of the three said.

Carter nodded slowly, his lips a tight line. "The Lex Talionis is mine." He got out of the Jeep and motioned the woman into place. Carter had to struggle to get the seat close enough for her legs to reach. "Head for the road, turn right, and keep going." He reached into the glove compartment and produced a large flashlight. "Use this when you have to." He showed them the weapons. "Use those if you have to." He picked up each piece and showed them how to remove the safety catch.

The three bankers got out of the car and bowed their thanks.

"Will you guys move it?" Carter said. "We'll have time for this later."

"You come to Japan?"

"I promise," Carter said.

"We will honor you when you come." They got back into the Jeep.

"I owe you," the young woman said.

Carter touched her cheek gently for a moment, then gave her an encouraging pat. "Move it," he said.

She engaged the gears expertly and moved smoothly down the turnoff toward the road. There was a coordinated sound of acceleration as the Jeep picked up momentum. She shifted through the gears as far as third by the time Zachary returned from his last sweep of the area. "They're off?"

Carter nodded.

"Good timing," Zachary said. "Looks like we got company."

# SEVENTEEN

The Jeep with the Japanese bankers was heading north and would soon angle to the northwest for a heading straight to Belmopan.

Two Jeeps edged their way up the road from the south. Carter estimated the Japanese bankers had a ten-minute head start. He made hand signals to indicate that Zachary get one of the arriving Jeeps. He'd take the other.

They waited in the thicket near the area where the disabled vehicles were parked. The important thing was to make sure the approaching Jeeps weren't in radio contact with anyone and didn't have transceivers. Otherwise, the entire force of Lex Talionis could be up there and all over them.

Carefully screwing a silencer onto Wilhelmina, Carter got the front tire of his Jeep just as the driver turned off the engine.

"Damn!" the driver cursed, killing the engine and hopping out. Two others followed him. "Hey, look at this," he shouted at the discovery that the other vehicles were disabled. "Something's going on here."

Zachary hit a tire of the second Jeep. The men in it spilled out. "What the hell's going on?" someone barked.

"I'll tell you what's wrong, those rice balls got away. And someone's still out there. Dammit, with all the men we've got, they can't guard these Japs properly."

Another voice complained, "Where the hell are a bunch of Japanese bankers going to go in this country? Use your head, man."

"That's the trouble. Too much thinking. When I was with the Marines, they put three men on small stuff, four on me-

147

dium stuff, and a whole platoon on big stuff. You think that guy, Calley, made first looey from his thinking? He knew how to use his fieldpiece, that's what."

Carter aimed at the men he'd chosen. He opened up before his men drew weapons. He popped the driver and a man with long mustaches. A third dropped to a crouch and took cover close to the incapacitated Jeep, fumbling at his holster to bring out a .45.

Zachary got one of his quarries, but the other two began to fan out in the darkness. Carter saw one, used a two-handed grip on Wilhelmina, and popped off a shot. Zachary's man groaned and fell. Carter wanted to make sure the survivors stayed out of the Jeeps, even though the vehicles were disabled. No use taking chances about radios.

Carter's survivor edged his way toward some of the other vehicles. The Killmaster pounced after him, diving under a Jeep and rolling through to the other side, grabbing his man by the ankle of his military boot and yanking. The guy went down, eating a bit of gravel and grass. Carter pounced on him, then finished him with Hugo.

Zachary had one survivor to go.

As Carter made his way back to the two new Jeeps, he heard a brief scuffle followed by a sharp intake of breath, then the sound of a body being lowered to the ground.

"All accounted for," Zachary said.

Carter shone his flash on the two Jeeps. Working quickly, he and Zachary removed the distributor rotors and tossed them into the underbrush. Carter also used Hugo to make a hash of the coolant hoses. One of the Jeeps had a radio, and Carter pumped four shots into it.

They went to the other vehicles and poured sand in the gas tanks. "Two hours," Carter said. "We bought them a two-hour lead. They won't get antsy and send someone to look for another two hours. If that doesn't get them out of here and to some kind of safety, nothing will."

Carter and Zachary took a hurried look around and decided to head back to the arts center. "They probably aren't in close contact with the center. I think that's just a big blind. We'll go back, get the car and our equipment, and take on some South African big game."

Zachary nodded, then started back on his own route. "I'll see what I can spot on the way."

Carter moved back through his assigned grids cautiously, looking for signs of trails, roadways, buildings, and vehicles. It was already four and dawn would be breaking soon; there was not very much time left. One of the last squares he could take before having to go back at a dead run had a particularly promising configuration: a small savannah amid the thinning forest. Beyond, Carter could hear running water in enough quantity to know that it was a stream that had been dammed.

Carter paused on the edge, knowing he had to risk it now that he was so close. If there were indeed some kind of building here, he'd head back the first thing tomorrow night when they were free from the constraints of their cover.

He started ahead but froze when he heard a rustling behind him.

Carter held his position, realizing he'd been meant to overhear his follower.

After a long pause, the rustling was heard again and a voice came out of the night. "Man, if you aren't something else, running that fancy grid pattern of yours. Where'd you learn that, man? Some Ivy League school?"

There was no scorn in the voice—far from it. Stepping out of the darkness to greet him and give him an affectionate embrace was Chepe Muñoz.

Before Carter could speak, the Cuban said, "I don't kill so easy, man, not when there's work to do."

Carter gave him a big grin. "What the hell happened back there in Mexico City, Chepe?"

"The bastards! They suckered me with hydrate in the beer. How they got it inside that fuckin' can beats me. Next thing you know I'm on some two-bit cargo plane, headin' wherever, you know? When we land, I returned the favor, suckered the guys right back. Those mothers think I'm trussed up all nice when I ain't, right? I bashed me some heads and did a fast fifteen hundred under three minutes and I'm gone, out of there, man."

Carter laughed at the idea of the big chunky Cuban running 1500 meters in world-record time.

Muñoz grinned back. "Hey, us big guys is all light on our feet, right? So I'm outta there, and I find me where I am—

Belize! So it's back on schedule and I been tracking the clowns this far. I was staking out those buildings waiting for the next patrol so I could tail it, when you guys come in and shoot the fuckin' place up."

"And they'll be after us soon," Carter said, "if we don't get back to the arts center. If Rogan is mixed up in LT, they'd have us spotted."

"I hear you, man. You guys had better get on back. I'll hang in here and tail the patrols. If I can get word out from their HQ, I will. If not I'll be there waiting for you. Just whistle. You know how to whistle, right, Carter?"

"If I don't, I'll learn."

Again Chepe Muñoz vanished back toward the shot-up buildings, and Carter faded into the night on a steady trot back to the Belize Center for the Arts.

Carter got back just before dawn, managed a scant two hours of sleep, got a shower, and was just working on a shave when Zachary knocked. The CIA man had brought them cups of coffee from his own stores. While Carter sipped, he filled Zachary in on the good news about Chepe Muñoz.

The shaggy-browed CIA man had a few things of his own to report. "Lots of signs of movement out there. Trucks, carryalls, troop transports."

"Were they going or coming?" Carter asked.

"We've got to assume they put the big guns out looking for the Japanese bankers."

Carter agreed. "This place, especially as the Center for the Arts, makes a great cover for all the activity, especially these festivals with people coming and going all the time. It looks like Rogan has sold his soul to keep this thing running, but I don't think he's necessarily one of the LT boys."

"It doesn't seem his style to be an active part of things," Zachary agreed. "But there is the matter of guilty knowledge."

Carter began assembling his things in a canvas bag. "The thing we have to look at carefully is our range of weapons. I have my Luger, a bit of ammo, and one put-together automatic. But I think we're going to need some heavy firepower."

Zachary shook his head. "I know what's coming. I'm not all that much better off. I have an AK-47, but I'm not overweight on ammo. I think we're going to have to assume it's out there and scrounge for it."

"We need some weaponry," Carter said. "If what we suspect is true, we need all the firepower we can get. It would also be good to have something for Chepe."

"Nothing like being forced into action," the CIA man said. "Let's go get some breakfast and tell Rogan we're on our way."

They both went to the cafeteria and had double orders of bacon and eggs, a sign to both that they were stoking for action and that the action was on its way.

Rogan did not like the fact that Carter and Zachary were heading back north, but he had what Zachary called a high-class problem. Even as they spoke, a bus filled with people arrived to participate in the festival. From the looks of them, they were mostly Americans. The gender balance went to women, many of whom were attractive middle-aged women, but some were much younger.

James Rogan was well aware of the new arrivals and he watched them, hopeful.

Sam Zachary picked up on the movement. "You must be at full capacity," he observed.

Rogan waved his hand. "We have a campground. We can handle even more."

"What about supplies?" Carter asked.

Rogan watched the Killmaster uneasily. "Were you ever a lawyer?"

Carter shook his head.

"You've got a way of asking questions that makes everything sound like an accusation."

"That makes it sound as if you've got something to be defensive about."

Rogan seemed to wince at that, but he decided to take the heat from Carter and allow the line of conversation to change. He continued to scan the new arrivals. "I wish you guys weren't taking off."

"We just came down here to broaden our horizons. It's time to move on." Carter extended his hand to Rogan who had no choice now but to take it, shake it, and, in so doing, let them off the hook.

"I sure wish you guys were staying," he said.

Carter and Zachary went to the car, did a quick security check on it, and judged it clean.

"You caught that he's expecting someone or something?" Carter said. "Someone with some money."

Another bus, smaller than the last, arrived at the front drive, discharging a number of men and women. Some appeared to have been at the arts center before. They got their luggage and moved purposefully to different parts of the campus, some to the area where Carter and Zachary were staying.

As the buses arrived, so did a six-wheel truck, filled with men in shiny new boots, olive drab trousers, and fatigue shirts. Carter pushed the point. "More of your guards?"

"I don't know what that is," Rogan said. "This is a big tract and we need security forces to keep our supplies intact. I have no idea what those guys want, but maybe some of the locals were trying to rip off some construction-grade lumber or maybe some of our canned food. They love canned food."

"I was thinking maybe they got a lead on those bombings," Carter said.

They left James Rogan standing nearby, watching the student arrivals and watching the handful of young soldiers, all of whom appeared to be in their teens, fanning out, trying to look friendly, but enjoying the uniforms and the drama of a search.

"You can be sure they're looking for those Japanese bankers. But I don't think Rogan's that far in on things. He thinks there's a courier bringing him money, but he doesn't know about the Japanese."

"I'm beginning to think that Rogan is not one of your all-time bright people."

They split off to attend to packing. As Carter neared his room, he became aware of a commotion heating up inside.

Pushing open the door, he saw Margo Huerta crouched in a fighting position. "You already had your chance," she said to someone in the room.

Wearing Levi's, an oversize cotton sweater, and Reebocks did nothing to hide the effect of Rachel Porat. Her eyes, locked on Margo Huerta, openly defied the larger woman. "You've returned at an interesting time, Carter," she said.

The Killmaster went directly to the small bureau where he

kept his things. "I could say the same for you, Rachel."

He opened drawers and began tossing his things into a canvas bag while the two women continued to stare one another down.

"Look at her, Carter," Rachel said, her voice dripping venom. "Is that the kind of woman who appeals to you? Or do you prefer someone who knows what you like and is able to provide it?"

"Bitch," Margo hissed and lunged at Rachel.

Rachel was waiting, and took advantage of Margo's lunge and her greater size, bringing her to the ground in a neatly executed side roll.

"Look at the way the cow falls," Rachel taunted, springing toward Margo, grabbing a handful of her hair. Margo got a grip on Rachel's left ankle, tugging until she brought Rachel down on top of her. The fighting became serious now as the women began grunting with exertion.

Carter moved in between them. "I should let you two fight it out, but I don't have the time or patience. We're into something vital here and the last thing I need is you two wasting energy over some ego."

Each woman responded by trying to seem sober and considerate. Rachel began caressing his shoulder. It had an immediate effect on him. Margo Huerta smiled and touched his hand provocatively. Carter stood looking at the pair when the knock came at the door. Before he could respond, Zachary entered, ready and eager.

"Far be it for me to give advice with my track record in relationships, but I'll tell you, tempting as it seems, that twosome stuff will cause you grief," Zachary said.

Carter motioned for both women to sit on the side of the bed. "We need a quick recap from you, Rachel. What brings you here?"

"What you would expect," Rachel Porat explained. "Piet Bezeidenhout. We know he is in this part of the world. This seems the most likely place to begin."

Carter turned his attention to Margo Huerta. "What have you discovered?"

"The seminars and festivals are serious enough. Rogan absolutely believes everything he says. But these festivals are also held as a cover for the tremendous amounts of supplies and food that come through here."

"Do you know where the receiving areas are?"

"I've found some, but there are more. It is said there is a large complex of warehouses nearby, well camouflaged."

Carter and Zachary exchanged glances. "It's time to get out of here and start pushing." He looked at Rachel. "We're after the same thing, only we're not just looking. We've got to take Bezeidenhout and his group apart. Are you with us?"

"I'm only supposed to look and report back," Rachel said. "Unless I get an unusual opportunity."

"You will," Carter promised. "Come on."

"And me?" Margo said. "Have all my efforts meant nothing just because I was willing to fight for you?"

"You've been a big help, but this is the separation point, the difference between dilettantism and professionalism. The three of us are professionals and know what's at risk."

"You think I know nothing of risk taking?" Margo was growing irate.

"I think you take risks, but we have to take them. We have no other profession to turn to."

"Let me come. I'll abide by your rules."

"Look at her, trying to curry favor," Rachel said.

Carter knew it was time for a decision. "Margo, you can stay with us as long as you follow the rules, but once one of us has reason to question you, it's over. Understood?"

Margo nodded solemnly. "This is for real."

Carter started to sketch copies of his map, but as he did, Rachel Porat reached into the hip pocket of her jeans. "This is one of the advantages of belonging to a group that has a famous uncle." She spread a large map of the area before them.

It was clear, detailed. "Where did you get this?" Zachary asked.

"An American stealth plane made a patterned flyover of this area for us, no questions asked. When we got the prints, we used a line-reduction printing and here it is, instant map, as accurate and recent as you can get."

Carter took the map and read appreciatively. "Some of these features are representations of buildings or camouflage configurations. This is going to make our lives a good deal easier." Using the Mossad map, Carter made rough copies for the others, giving the proper compass orientation and grids.

Zachary was amazed. "I probably couldn't get one of these if I asked for it, and I work for them."

"Let's get moving," Carter said. He established reconnaissance areas for each of them, and assigned check-in times and signals. Then he and Zachary took their things to the car.

Rachel Porat and Margo Huerta were still working under cover identities. Margo still had the guise of a volunteer at the arts center. Rachel was a new arrival on the bus, presumably there for the festival activity. It was now up to each woman to get away on her own without being noticed.

Carter and Zachary loaded the car and headed out the long circular drive, honking to some persons they recognized, heading for all intents and purposes back to Belmopan.

After about three miles of travel down the road, Carter found an area of jungle and overhang that suited his purpose for safely storing the car. He pulled over, removed the necessary equipment, and began to work. He and Zachary put in nearly an hour, erecting a suitable hiding place. They both knew that a car left by the side of the road in country like this would be considered abandoned or fair game. What was left in good faith could very well be missing in a country where there are not many big opportunities.

Each man rigged himself to carry as much equipment as possible, fashioning the equivalents of field packs. Zachary shared some of his water purifying pills with Carter.

The two men had a final cigarette from Carter's case, then turned and melted into the jungle. They were on their way to find Lex Talionis.

# EIGHTEEN

After a fast march of over an hour, Nick Carter reached the point on his grid maps where he believed the hospital setup of Dr. Charles Smith was located. Now he began fanning out in circles, looking for traces of roads, utility lines or outbuildings for generators or propane gas containers.

The path, when he found it, was quite sophisticated, made of ground-up saplings and vines. It led Carter to a large building the size of an airplane hangar at a small airport, no great shakes in construction, but sturdy for the job. There were rib and truss beams forming an arc, mounted on top of a large square. Mounted on the outside of the large building were four large air conditioners. A quarter mile or so from the large building was a cinder-block building of about a hundred square feet. Carter had no trouble getting a look inside. His suspicions were confirmed: in it were three large generators and several drums of fuel.

There were only two signs on the large building, PRIVATE and NO UNAUTHORIZED ADMISSION. There were no indications of guards or campsites. As he circled closer, Carter did find a construction that convinced him Dr. Smith liked fresh flowers. A small greenhouse flourished in the tropical growth. Moving in for a closer look, Carter saw an interesting assortment of fuscias, begonias, and bright, cheery asters.

Poking closer to the main building, Carter got a look in a window and saw what was probably a nurse's quarters. At the next level of window, he saw what he had hoped to discover: a small room, well appointed with a hospital bed. Lying in the bed was a man whose face was swathed in bandages. Something familiar about the man tugged at Carter. It was Bud

Gonder, the young student from the infirmary and the bomb explosion. Dr. Charles Smith apparently couldn't resist the challenge of giving people different appearances.

There were two other recovery rooms, but each was empty at the moment.

Carter did a quick tour around the building and saw nothing to spoil his earlier assessment about any kind of security system. He looked carefully for electronic alarms, found none, and decided he was going to take his chances by mounting the small four-step tier to the building and stepping inside.

He'd been in dozens of similar buildings, the walls painted in institutional colors and the lobby filled with regulation furniture. A series of doors led to small storage rooms, a nurse's lounge, and a small library with a computer hookup for data base research. A slightly larger door led to an impressive wood-paneled office about twenty feet square. There was a large mahogany desk, teak shelves, and a number of pre-Columbian artifacts. On the desk were several boxes of Cuban cigars. There were also a few large boxes of granola bars. Anticipating the hunger that would soon be on him, Carter took two bars.

Carter guessed this luxurious enclave was Dr. Charles Smith's office when he was in residence. It had the look, the smell, and the tone of a man who thought well of himself and wanted all his outward accoutrements to reflect the fact.

Next to the office was a small, deluxe room with wood paneling, some first-rate graphics on the walls, a water bed, and an expensive stereo system with large, boxy speakers. Without spending too much time checking out meaningless details, Carter saw that there was a large modular shower and a full-length triple mirror. Dr. Smith traveled in style.

The thing Carter wanted to see next was down at the end of the hall, another large room, probably the same twenty-by-twenty dimension as Smith's office. This was the operating room, a first-class setup with a bank of overhead mercury vapor lamps, an adjustable table, long banks of X-ray readers, a huge autoclave for sterilizing instruments, a large wooden cabinet with several drawers, and, finally, a huge glass cabinet filled with an array of knives, saws, drills, chisels, and other surgical tools. Lit by fluorescent wall fixtures for the times when the mercury vapors were not on, the room was a well-organized, efficient operating room.

Carter wondered if the Grinning Gaucho hadn't had his identity laundered in this very room.

The sound of nurses talking from a nearby room caused Carter to duck toward the door, but there he was met by the diminutive, cigar-smoking doctor, dressed now in stone-washed denims and running shoes. "The curiosity got to you, right?" he said.

Carter decided to tough it out by saying nothing.

"I can promise you, there will be little or no pain at any time." He began to scan Carter's face. "It's a shame to do any work on a face like yours. You've got classic features. Good bones. Well, come on over here and let's get started."

"I think you have the wrong idea," Carter said.

The doctor became irate. "I think *you* have the wrong idea." He pulled the cigar from his mouth and heaved it forcefully. "Dammit, you'd think they'd do some kind of a briefing first." He stared at Carter. "You think I'm just going to sedate you and start cutting, right, fellow? Jeez, gimme a break. I take something like six hundred different measurements, some within a tenth of a millimeter. Then I build a topography—here, I'll show you." He moved to the large wooden cabinet and opened it, removing what looked to Carter like a death mask.

"It's called a moulage," the doctor said, extending a plaster cast toward Carter. "We're talking exquisite detail here, so don't go backing away like I was going to start cutting you right now. Hell, you can't know it, but you're getting the best. I give you features you'd never dream of." He studied Carter for a few moments. "I can fix it so your jaw will never pop again. You'll be free of that, you understand."

"Those casts are all of people you worked on?"

"Damned right," the doctor said. "That's just responsibility to keep track. Those bozos in the CIA are scared stiff someone is going to find my records and then everyone will recognize you." He snorted. "Hell, when I'm through with you, no one will recognize you."

Carter edged toward the door. "Thanks, but I think there's been a misunderstanding."

"I'm telling you," the doctor said, "*you're* doing the misunderstanding. I just want to measure you first. Don't even think about surgery for a week or so. Now, be reasonable. Let's get on with the measurements."

Carter backed toward the door.

"That tears it," the doctor said. "Bruno! Marvin! I got a stubborn one here. Doesn't want to be measured."

The door opened and two men entered, both well over six four. One of them was black, his head shaven clean, a Puerto Vallarta T-shirt looking incongruous on his enormous frame. The other was a prototype of a wide receiver, blond, powerful, fast. They came at Carter. "Easy does it, buddy," the black guy said and extended his hand. "Doc here just wants to take some measurements with a small little ruler."

He feinted at Carter, who did not take the bait at all. "Let's cut this nonsense right now," Carter said.

"Hey, buddy, you let the doc measure you and we got no problems," the black guy said, reaching quickly for Carter and getting his hand. The Killmaster spun away, bumping the big blond off-balance. Carter danced back toward the black, elbowed him in the gut, and dropped into a crouch to take the charge from the blond.

Carter sidestepped that, tripped the blond, and was at the door. Both men were stunned with surprise. The black started at Carter again, driving him back against the blond, who got Carter in a bear hug, but Carter immediately shot his feet into the black guy's chest, dropping him and spinning away from the blond.

"I don't want to have to do this," Carter said.

The blond guy was out to save face. All seriousness now, he reached for Carter, who got a hand on the sleeve of his smock, tugged, and brought him to his knees with a crash. Frustrated, the blond got to his feet with some fancy gymnastics and came at Carter.

"What the hell is this?" the doctor shouted. "From now on, they're all going to sign releases before they come to me. I've had it with this skittishness."

The blond threw a punch at Carter who caught it in his left hand, squeezed, twisted, and wrenched the man to the floor with a hard slam.

Carter was out of the room, down the steps, and out into

the jungle as quickly as possible, the irate voice of Dr. Charles Smith bawling at the two goons.

Using his copy of the Mossad map, Carter oriented himself and set off at an angle across the vast expanse of jungle on the far side of the Center for the Arts. He moved at a fast pace for nearly an hour before he paused for a cigarette.

A nearby stream ran high with fresh water. He drank his fill, then immersed his canteen. Coming back to his compass heading, Carter began to notice a thinning of the forest and his instincts began to play on him. Without knowing why at first, he began a crosshatch pattern, putting in a good deal of time to cover very little territory, but as he rounded the next bend, he saw the fruits of his instinctive labors. Before him, curling out of the forest, was a well-graded road.

Heading in a northeasterly direction, Carter followed the road, having to duck quickly off the side of the road when a Jeep with two armed men drove by. About ten minutes later another vehicle appeared, a classic VW bug that had been converted into a Baja buggy, complete with thick-tread tires, a long looping antenna, and halide lights for running in the darkness off the beaten path.

There was no longer any question about it: the Killmaster knew he was coming closer to the real quarry.

A half hour later another vehicle passed, pausing to scan the sides of the road. This one, a large-bed Toyota pickup, was relatively new and smeared with camouflage. Two men rode in the cab, and an armed man sat in the bed with an automatic weapon.

Carter couldn't tell if they were merely on patrol or specifically looking for him, but after more time had elapsed he began to hear a steady, droning sound in the distance.

The droning appeared to come closer, then ebb. Carter couldn't figure out what it was until he mounted a small hillock and the afternoon breeze brought him the sound, clear, unhampered. It was someone broadcasting a message through a battery-powered bull horn.

A mile down the road on Carter's right was a small pathway. The area was definitely filled with signs of life now, and Carter knew that every step he took was bringing him into the middle of things. He took the pathway and there, in a clearing, were two added traces that an army was in residence. On one side of the clearing was a firing range, with bunkers, sandbags, and targets. On the other ws a fitness range, with ropes for swinging, a crawling range, and an obstacle course made from old tires and empty barrels. Someone was interested in military training, military discipline. Carter made a quick sweep through the firing range. There were some casings from the older, more conventional rifles, but there were even more spent casings from automatic weapons.

The droning sound of the bull horn came closer, and overhead, Carter heard the unmistakable sound of a chopper flying a search pattern.

A half mile down the road, Carter ducked into the bushes in time to avoid being spotted by a Jeep. Unlike the other vehicles he'd seen, this one was almost new and had a logo stenciled on the side door. LT, the logo read.

Lex Talionis.

Carter had arrived.

He approached a rise in the road and saw that he had now come to a point where there was an intersection running in an east-west direction. There were also indications of more foot trails.

One particular trail was well packed, topped with gravel. Carter decided to try it, starting out just as another vehicle with a bull horn came by. The words were in English, but he could still not make them out.

At the end of the dirt path, Carter saw two armed guards seated in a small hut, one reading a wrestling magazine, the other trimming his fingernails with a knife. Carter spotted a powerful transceiver in the foreground. These men might not inspire military respect, but they were out there, they were armed, and they had the ability to communicate with at least one other source.

It took Nick Carter another hour of stealthy moving through the thinning jungle to see what was so important.

Climbing nearly a quarter mile in altitude, Carter stood at the side of an outcropping and looked down at a large reservoir. It was man-made, the roads packed and graded. No more than three feet over the surface of the reservoir were a series of camouflage nets, making it all but impossible for the water to be seen from above. Carter paused to check the Mossad map. Detailed and sophisticated as it was, it had fooled the camera. Lex Talionis was apparently equipped with all the essentials for survival and for avoiding detection.

As Carter dropped back down to the intersection, he became aware of the sound of the bull horn blasting its message.

Pausing to listen, he could pick out an occasional word as the Jeep came rumbling closer. "... amnesty ... guest ... hospitality ... we will take no hostile action ..."

The pounding, thwacking sound of a chopper beat through the jungle. Carter could hear it flying search patterns at a low altitude. Another of the VW Baja buggies came careening down the road, oversize tires biting into the dirt. The driver was young, but seated in front, holding a Kalashnikov at port arms, an older man in uniform looked battle-weary from all the wars he'd been in and not from any one in particular.

Carter listened to the message a bit longer, trying to piece more of it together. At first he'd thought it was merely some propaganda for a group of locals, but then he'd begun to realize that the message was for him. The people with the bull horn were calling him by name! Then he heard other names being mentioned: Chepe Muñoz and Sam Zachary.

The voice on the bull horn was careful about the way it explained things. Nothing like "we have your comrades." This was tactful and friendly.

"Mr. Nick Carter, we invite you to join us. We have nothing to hide. Your friends have taken our hospitality. You may keep your weapons if you wish. That is not an issue. We merely wish to make you a gentlemanly offer."

Carter continued toward where he believed he would find the main concentration of LT.

The bullhorn persisted for nearly an hour, and with the chopper running its search pattern, Carter found it necessary to stay off the road, paralleling its course and keeping cover.

Nearly an hour later, the LT people resorted to another stratagem. As Carter hid off the main road, a Jeep moved slowly along. With the exception of the driver, who wore a holster at his waist, none of the other passengers was armed. It was the persons sitting in back who most interested Carter.

Smoking a cigar and looking comfortable in the deepening afternoon was Chepe Muñoz. Sitting next to him, waving away the fumes, was Sam Zachary. Neither man looked to be under the slightest duress.

Zachary motioned the driver to a halt and took up the bull horn. He identified himself and asked Carter to come forth. "They'll even let us have a hostage," Zachary said. "I'm convinced they're only interested in talk right now."

Carter did not like the idea of giving up an advantage, not when he was getting so close to the mark. Not when Bezeidenhout was likely to suspect they'd been responsible for the loss of so much money in the form of the Japanese investment bankers.

"Strictly on the up-and-up, Carter. If you come in, we can meet Bezeidenhout within the hour."

Carter was close enough to hear Zachary and Muñoz talking.

"I say we can stand here and offer things until doomsday, but Nick Carter won't give up an advantage," Zachary said.

"So what do we do? These *pendejos* won't wait all year, *compadre*. And they said they wanted to talk to him, too."

"We take them at their word and talk to them," Zachary said. "We get all the information we can, and then we use our opportunities."

"And Carter?"

Zachary spoke with admiration. "Surely you realize by now that all Carter ever does is use his opportunities."

Zachary motioned the driver on and the jeep sped along into the lengthening afternoon.

Carter took a swig of water from his canteen and kept moving. He trusted Zachary and Muñoz, but they had their approaches and he had his. There was no question in his mind that he, too, would see Piet Bezeidenhout, but on his terms.

# NINETEEN

Carter walked until darkness began to fall. He came to a large bunker that served as a jungle supply dump. It was chained shut, locked in place. Carter took care of the lock with one silenced shot from Wilhelmina. In the process, he found an automatic weapon and several clips of ammunition. He also found rope and bandoleers for carrying ammunition.

A new carton of bayonets left him uninterested. Breaking one out of its Pliofilm and grease preservative, Carter found it all but useless. Even though a knife was a treasure in terrain like this, these would require hours of honing and treating.

Set off in the corner against a wall of canned foods, grenade launchers, and an obsolete mortar, Carter saw a little NR-6 two-banger motorcycle with the heavy-treaded wheels needed for this kind of road. There was a small amount of fuel in the tank, but searching around the bunker, he found a large metal can of gas. He filled up the NR-6 and started kicking at the pedal.

The cycle flooded. Carter had to drain and then prime it, but finally it began with a steady roar. So much for any secrecy, but he'd take care of that when the problem arose.

Riding the NR-6 for another twenty minutes, Carter came to the top of a rise where he saw the area where Zachary and Muñoz had undoubtedly been taken. There were several large barracks-type buildings, a motor pool, and one large Quonset hut with two pumps in front, probably one diesel, the other gas.

He left the cycle and continued on foot, stopping from time to time to check on a suspicion that was growing. Someone was tracking him. He already had an idea who, but not why.

Hacking off a generous length of rope, he made a noose trap in a grassy glade, triggering the device with a young sapling. He led his tracker in a circle, back through the glade, carefully retracing his own tracks.

After a few moments, he heard a voice swear in the guttural street Arabic of Beirut. "Shit! Oldest damned trick in the world and I fall for it!"

Carter found his quarry hanging by his left foot, trying to reach his knife. The Killmaster quickly intercepted the knife and stuck it in his own belt. The man's gun had fallen well out of his reach.

He found himself looking at a sullen young man, barely twenty. "I thought I was pretty good, surviving a lot of stuff with the Israelis and those goddamned militiamen, and so what do I do but walk into the classic trap of all time."

"Happens to all of us," Carter said in Palestinian Arabic.

"You?" the kid asked.

"No," Carter said. "Luck, I guess."

"Sure! Luck!" The young man spat. He had lost considerable face but was smart enough to know that in his current position, no amount of posturing or swearing was going to make things any better for him.

"How many of you are there with Samadhi?" Carter asked.

The kid shook his head. "You're so good, you tell me."

"Six or eight."

The kid nodded.

"How'd you get over?"

"Abdul sent for us. The others were taken out in Mexico. Some action in the mountains."

"Are there more of you on the way?"

The kid nodded. "Every time Abdul gets money, he sends for more."

"So Abdul has a jihad against LT?"

"Are you going to kill me?"

"No," Carter said, "not if you answer my questions."

Carter tossed the kid his own knife. By the time he got himself free, he was grateful to accept a cigarette. "These Lex Talionis pigs, they burned the PLO for a lot of money. Abdul says they'll pay for it. He means to get it back."

"You guys did the bombs back at the arts center?"

"Those were good, weren't they? I made those."

"Someone could have been hurt," Carter said.

"I'm telling you, I know what I'm doing." It suddenly dawned on the kid that Carter was probably American. "Who do you work for?"

"You never heard of them," Carter said. "For the moment, we're on the same side."

"We're not on anyone's side," the kid said, "except our own."

"I want you to take a message to Samadhi for me. Will you do that? Will you tell him it's from the Killmaster?"

"Is that your street name?"

"You could say that, yes. I want you to tell Samadhi that Lex Talionis took three hostages, Japanese."

"Hell, we know that."

"Yes, but do you know I let them go?"

"You got a huge ransom."

Carter shook his head. "I got nothing."

The kid looked at Carter, unbelieving. "You let hostages go? For nothing?"

Carter nodded. "There is now a fifty-fifty chance that Lex Talionis thinks you guys did it."

"We wouldn't have let them go. That's big money. Weapons. Political pressure."

"I'm warning you," Carter said. "Be careful. And one more thing. Stay out of my way. Can I trust you to tell these things to Samadhi?"

"Sure,"the kid said, feeling full of himself again.

"How do I know you'll tell him?"

"An American who speaks Arabic like you, you think I'd miss a chance to tell about that?"

"I think you might be more likely to have to explain if I took your Nikes."

The kid looked down at his shoes.

Carter made a motion with Wilhelmina.

The kid had to show Carter it was no big thing. He took off his Nikes and scornfully tossed them off to the side.

"How old are you?"

"Sixteen."

"You're not sixteen."

"Well, they all take me for sixteen."

Probably closer to fourteen, Carter thought, giving the kid

his gun back. The world was tough in a lot of places. Lebanon. Nicaragua. Peru. But Carter still thought fourteen was too young for that kind of growing up. "Get going," he said, "and watch out for snakes."

The kid's eyes met Carter's as if to say he'd been in worse scrapes in Beirut, and Carter believed he actually had, but the Killmaster had worried him with the bit about the snakes.

Carter waved Wilhelmina at him and he started off gingerly through the forest. Carter knew that before long, some young Lex Talionis recruit was going to be minus a pair of boots and this Arab kid was going to show up with a pair of field shoes that stood out from the Nikes and Reeboks of his companions. All of which was exactly what Carter was counting on.

Two hours later Carter penetrated what he thought was the main LT compound. A series of barracks-like buildings was grouped around a large outdoor amphitheater. By working his way past the sentries on post, Carter moved from building to building until he heard Chepe Muñoz's voice. Rubbing dirt on his face, Carter risked a look in the window. There was Muñoz, seated at a table, smoking a cigar. In the room with him was a blond man of medium height wearing gold-rimmed glasses. He wore olive drab pants and shirt, and a duck-billed cap. Carter could tell by his high, nasal accent that he was a South African.

Piet Bezeidenhout.

Pulling one of the flat, miniaturized devices from his wallet, Carter was able to get a good fix on the conversation inside without having to risk showing himself.

"I know you, Muñoz. I know your work, your ability to inspire men. Think what it could do for our operation if you would come over and join us."

"Hey, man," Muñoz said, "twenty-five years of Cuban revolution may not be the most stable kind of job security in the world, but you cats are just starting and you've got nothing solid to hold you together."

"Ah, but that's the beauty of it," Bezeidenhout insisted. "There is everything a man like you could want. Incentives. Opportunities. My plan is the essence of capitalistic invention. There have been some enormous companies based on the so-called multilevel structure. We are beholden to no creed or political calling except our own. We are the fighting man's equivalent of the think tank. In what army can a man reinvest his own earnings? Be one of my captains, Chepe, and by year's end, you will be a wealthy, satisfied man."

"Where is all this money coming from?" Muñoz asked.

"Good you ask. That is practical. I have a client list."

"Clients?"

"People. Groups who are willing to pay large sums of money to have events take place."

"Terrorist events, Bezeidenhout?"

"Events of magnitude. Events that will draw the attention of the rest of the world. Soon there will be thousands of men in an elite corps. The finest from around the world. Men living and working here, working under the brotherhood of power. Lex Talionis. The law of the lion. It will be outlaw and it will be fitting because we are located in the jungle. But in the jungle there will be condominiums. Each who joins us will own his own home. There will be all the amenities appropriate for such a good cadre."

"In this brotherhood of yours, Bezeidenhout, will there be any black leaders?"

"Why do you dwell on such foolishness?"

"Because you come from a place where there's a lot of that very kind of foolishness."

"In Lex Talionis, my men will advance strictly on merit. If a black man brings in significant customers, he will surely profit. If he is willing to take great risks, he will be given greater rewards."

"I've been in politics a long time now," Muñoz said, "and it's my observation that you sound like one of these operations where you've got maybe two, three barracudas and a goldfish in the same tank. With all that tension and pressure, someone's going to get the goldfish for dinner, but as far as you're concerned, the barracudas can knock each other off for the privilege."

"Bah, don't be so stubborn with your talk of politics and folk-tale wisdom. Listen to me, Chepe Muñoz. Here is my offer. Choose your currency. Swiss francs. Japanese yen. Dollars. Krugerrands. I guarantee you two thousand a month as a base cover. Even if you do nothing, you bring in that much. But when you, as one of my captains, bring in other income, you will have a seventeen-and-a-half-percent share. You see how it works?" Bezeidenhout began reading off a list. "Taking hostage an oil sheik from OPEC. Mining the harbor at Sydney, Australia. Placing bombs in the Boulder Dam in Nevada. Ah, here, mining the dikes in the Netherlands. These are all lucrative offers, made by people who stand to gain something from them."

"I see that you gave up your position with the diamond cartel for the opportunity to work with a bunch of losers and bozos."

"Bozos?"

"An expression, Bezeidenhout, that shows a lack of thinking at crucial times."

"So you are refusing my offer?"

"Hey," Chepe Muñoz intoned, "did I say that, man? You just got to give me more time to think about it, right? Tell you what, I'll head back to Cuba, chew it over with Doc Fidel, okay?"

The South African looked at him coldly. "Your humor is as twisted as your politics, Muñoz. Guards, here! Take this man away and lock him up. Tomorrow, after we deal with Zachary and Carter, we'll decide what to do with him."

Smiling, Chepe Muñoz was marched out of the room. Carter slipped into the night and lay waiting. When the squad of baby-faced LT soldiers marched the burly Cuban out and turned toward a stout cinder-block building, Carter opened fire. He picked off two of the guards before they were aware they were being fired upon. The other four, as he'd expected, hit the ground in panic, leaving Chepe Muñoz momentarily forgotten. The big Cuban moved like a scalded cat and was almost to the cover of the first building before the guards knew he'd moved.

"The prisoner!"

"Get him, you jerks!"

All four scrambled up to chase the Cuban, forgetting Carter. The Killmaster cut down two more with two slow shots. The remaining two clawed for the dirt again. Before they even raised their heads, Muñoz vanished into the shadows, and Carter was a hundred yards away on his original quest. Chepe Muñoz would take care of himself. It was time to find Zachary. He continued his survey of the buildings in the compound but was not successful in locating the shaggy-browed CIA man. Had they finished him off? Carter wondered. Taken him to another compound?

He started due east, looking for the site of another reservoir on the Mossad map. It might give him a good idea when the time came to take this place off the map. It also gave him an opportunity to estimate the number of LT forces in the area. So far, he figured close to six hundred.

There was indeed another compound and Carter saw the outline in the dark. He started making his way toward it, but he was stopped by the sound of shooting.

The shooting was coming from the south, handguns and automatic weapons. Carter had no idea who the combatants were. For all he knew, it could be the young Arab kid from the Samadhi group, trying to win his honor and some shoes back.

Carter got as close to the exchange of fire as possible, moving from the shelter of trees and low shrubs. He got out his infrared scope and tried to get a fix, but he was too far away to see anything

He moved in closer, using the sounds of the gunfire to cover his less controlled movements. Taking out the scope again, he got a fix on two Lex Talionis soldiers with automatic weapons.

They had someone pinned down who was nevertheless doing a good job of keeping them hopping, driving them back, forcing them to move away from higher ground.

One of the LT soldiers tried to do a flanking maneuver and got grazed on the left shoulder for his efforts.

Carter tripped over a snag and drew fire himself from the individual the LT men were shooting at. He decided it was time to get out of there, circle back, and see if he could discover who it was these LT were after.

Moving in a low crouch, he heard a familiar voice he could not place, swearing in the night, then there was another furious burst of fire and a scramble of feet over gravel and rocks. Carter heard two more LT men arriving from a westerly direction. They were counting on surprise, moving on their stomachs, looking as if they'd done two, three hundred hours in some commando course. They gained their position by stealth, but when they opened up fire, all they did was tear a tree to shreds. Their quarry had evaded them, done a half circle, and gained some high ground over the other two LT. A barrage of shots caught one of the surprised LT men and dropped him cold.

Whoever it was they were after, he knew his way around in a fight, and it was beginning to look as if he might be able to take all four of the LT.

Then Carter heard the familiar, guttural voice swear and saw a handgun thrown in disgust. The three surviving LT figured they had their prey trapped. They opened up on him. One of them, a big guy with a pencil-thin mustache, was surprised beyond measure. Another handgun sounded, catching Mustache in the chest. The LT boys were down to two, nervous and frustrated. They had a lot of shells and didn't mind shooting it up.

Carter got in close enough to get his scope out and see what was happening. The LT men were equipped with Kalashnikovs. They had the quarry at bay now, although the way they were going at it, there was a good possibility they'd get each other in their carelessness.

They opened fire, wasting a lot of ammo. Carter saw their quarry and admired the fight he'd put up. Even while taking a hit from one of the assault rifles, he raised up, used a two-handed grip, and popped off two quick shots that took one of the LT men.

The surviving LT was really caught up in it, stitching fire back and forth over everything in sight. Then it was all over. One young LT soldier was left, panting, charged with adrenaline and fear, already thinking how he was going to present his story. It had taken four of them to get Chepe Muñoz.

Still panting, the surviving LT came charging down to where Chepe lay and began pulling out his knife.

Carter used the infrared scope to take careful aim with Wilhelmina. It was by necessity a one-handed grip. Carter held his breath, and pulled off one shot. Wilhelmina barked sharply in the night.

The LT man's howl of rage and surprise rang out as he went pitching facedown near the man whose corpse he'd been about to mutilate.

Carter couldn't tell if there was any life in Muñoz or not. He stood near the Cuban for a moment. "Good to know you, *amigo*," he said. "I haven't forgotten our pact. I'll get them."

Now Carter had enough weapons and ammunition. He didn't have to bother checking the LT corpses.

# TWENTY

Nick Carter was carefully examining the buildings in the next compound, hoping to find a trace of Zachary.

Bezeidenhout could have made it a major goal to get the CIA man to come over to Lex Talionis. LT could have made Zachary an offer. And Zachary, wealthy in his own right, would have laughed and that apparently was something you did not do with Bezeidenhout. You didn't laugh at him, and you didn't ignore his offers.

Carter could be in this by himself now.

He got past a patrolling sentry and made a bolt for a place about a hundred yards from some buildings. There were three or four trees including one rotted stump, which was just right for Carter's purpose. Cupping his hands carefully, he lit a cigarette and let the smoke run in the stump. He'd covered half the buildings in the compound and had decided which one he'd look at next before he moved out.

When he heard the whistling sound, he nearly laughed aloud. He took one last puff of his cigarette, ground it out, and carefully destroyed all traces of it. By that time, a loud thump had landed on one of the buildings Carter had already checked. The thump caused a small explosion and a lot of thick, white smoke. Another whistle and another projectile hit the building.

Carter was positive it was Samadhi and his boys, hitting at the LT camp.

Men ran from the shed, waving away smoke, grabbing at weapons. One more shell arced from its firing position, slammed into the shed, and caused the biggest explosion so far.

Carter heard a good deal of yelling in Spanish, French, and English. Lex Talionis men were trying to form a group and start some kind of counterattack.

A shell hit another building in the roof and got enough of a fire going so that Carter thought he'd better get some distance. Even though there was general confusion, it made no sense to take the chance of being seen by patrols. He headed down to the farthest of the sheds he'd wanted to check out. Gunfire erupted and for a moment he found himself caught in a hail of shots, but a last shell took a building squarely on the roof, filled it with smoke, and produced a shattering blast.

Carter could see as many as twenty LT men, weapons out, firing at everything that moved. To his right, someone yelled, "Here it is! Those pigs had a grenade launcher and a bazooka!"

By the burning or smoking buildings, a number of men, unfamiliar with chemical fire extinguishers, were trying to put out the fires that had been started. The air was filled with smoke and pungent smells. One shed must have contained ammunition. It was rocked by a series of explosions that destroyed all the internal support. The room came pitching in, sending more sparks and flames into the night sky.

As Carter neared the back building, he heard a commotion. "Hey, come here! You aren't supposed to leave yet. The boss still wants to talk to you. There's more stuff to look at."

A figure appeared in the window, did a roll tuck, and hit through the frame with a shower of glass. Sam Zachary landed outside, brushed some of the glass from his shoulders, and started moving.

"Hey! I've got to shoot if you don't stop!"

"Shoot away," Zachary called. "I'm not stopping."

There were two warning shots fired at Zachary, but he didn't stop or look back. Carter angled toward him, ducked beside a building, found a rock, and tossed it. The rock caught Zachary's attention. He looked up, saw Carter, and smiled. "I don't have any weapons."

"Later," Carter said. "We'll get you some."

They put about half a mile between them and the activity back at the compound before stopping to catch up.

"I take it they made you an offer," Carter said.

"We hadn't reached that point yet," Zachary explained.

"Bezeidenhout wanted me to see the operation. He was coming on slow, trying to impress me with all the resources. He also thought I'd be a good minister in the field. Expense accounts. Travel. Seeing a lot of potential customers. I think he had Chepe pegged as his man in the field."

"How come they had you and Chepe separated?"

"Psychology. If one of us went, then the other would be likely. Same tricks as when you go in to buy a new car."

"Not quite," Carter said, and he told Zachary how Muñoz had bought it from the LT.

Zachary watched him for a moment. "Screw it, let's go get 'em."

"I'm way ahead of you," the Killmaster said.

"My vote," Zachary said, "is that we finish up with what we started this morning. Let's knock as many vehicles out of commission as we can."

Carter agreed. They spread out the Mossad map and set two rendezvous points.

"As far as I'm concerned," Zachary said, "the only reason for bringing Bezeidenhout in will be if he doesn't get hurt on the way. You follow me?"

Carter nodded. "I'd like to talk to him if possible. Get some details squared away." Another muffled explosion sounded in the distance. "You may notice an occasional bit of help from Abdul Samadhi," Carter said. "He's after his own revenge and his own justice." He gave Zachary his automatic and a bandoleer of shells, then started back to see what was left of the compound that had been bombarded by Samadhi and his band.

Uniformed LT men were having trouble bringing the fire under control, getting the debris set aside, and trying to keep the flames away from anything explosive. Carter could see the problem. Some of the officers might have made it to the rank of sergeant in some armies, but they were clearly not lieutenants or captains, standing there, berating their men and shouting louder and louder.

Carter circled his way back to one of the larger motor pools. Here, he had to begin making contact with the guards. There were about twelve of them in varying degrees of walking patrol, maintaining surveillance over a sector of the park, and, in one case, performing actual repairs on a command car.

The Killmaster brought Hugo out and went at the most remote of the guards, over by the large troop transports. Carter got the man squarely in the neck and quickly hefted the body into the back of one of the large transports.

He cut the fuel lines on two of the large vehicles and moved on to the next guard, whom he was able to overcome with a neck pinch and finally a sharp rabbit punch. Taking no chances, Carter used the man's belt and his bandoleer to secure him. The man's automatic weapon made a good substitute for the one Carter had given to Zachary. Carter helped himself to pockets full of clips.

He decommissioned two trucks and a Jeep, cut fuel lines on another, and now began to approach two of the VW Baja buggies. A guard sat asleep in one and Carter decided he'd pushed his luck as much as possible. He doubled back to the farthest point he'd worked, ran some rags through spilled fuel, thumbed his lighter, and produced a torch.

Two trucks caught immediately and the trail of fuel led quickly to others, the burning fuel beginning to make a roar. Someone noted the flames and began shouting. Soon there were others taking up the cry. Carter paused to watch until it became clear that there was going to be a lot of damage, then he melted away from the light and started toward the main compound where he'd overheard the conversation between Bezeidenhout and Chepe Muñoz.

He cut carefully through the open-air amphitheater and came back to the large barracks. Movement was more difficult now. The LT cadres were out in force organizing patrols.

Inching his way to the side of the building, he placed his listening device against a wooden slat. The device immediately brought in the sound of a familiar voice. "We are sincerely pleased to have you with us, even though there seem to be some minor disturbances."

"Sounds to me like your security system isn't so hot for an organization your size." The voice belonged to Rachel Porat, and there was a note of scorn in her tone.

Piet Bezeidenhout was not flapped. "There are a lot of loose ends to be ironed out for an organization this large, but I can assure you I have a powerful security committee. Anders Koven, my chief, has been with some of the major multinational organizations."

Rachel Porat hooted in derision. "Apparently Abdul Samadhi can come into your encampment and raise hell whenever he chooses. It makes me wonder why an organization as good as yours is supposed to be can't handle a small gang of PLO. It also makes me wonder what you could possibly have that would interest us." Rachel was really pouring it on now. "Why should we pay Lex Talionis for a number of things we could do cheaper and better ourselves?"

"You see," Bezeidenhout said, "you forgot the obvious. If you want something of sensitivity or delicacy done, you must be positive in advance that your security is excellent and that there are no traitors. When your people, for instance, eliminated Abu Jihad—"

"There is no proof whatsoever that we were involved with that," Rachel protested.

Bezeidenhout laughed. "All the world is the proof, my dear lady. There is not a country in the world that doesn't think you people did that, simply because you didn't deny it at the proper time. But look, let's get to some specifics. We have within the Lex Talionis two of the most elite action squads. One is, at this very moment, headed to the North Sea to arrange an event on an oil platform. I can tell you no more than that because of security reasons, but when the worldwide headlines break, you will say to yourself, 'I was told by the head of Lex Talionis about this very event.'"

"Go on," Rachel Porat said.

"My second action squad is about to cause aviation history. There will be a disaster—a tragedy, you might say—and a major manufacturer of passenger aircraft will be discredited to the detriment of its market position." There was a moment of pause, and Carter wished he could see the Israeli spy's expression.

"I see your scorn plainly on your face, but look at the Americans and their defense department scandals. Big money is at stake here, with organizations willing to do drastic things to achieve their long-range goals."

"So get to the point," Rachel said.

"The point is that I ask you to join me. There are not many good women in your profession. You will go far."

"And live here, amidst all these dregs of humanity who can get jobs in no other way other than to sell their very souls?"

"My dear, you don't understand. This is to be the main base of Lex Talionis, but there is no reason to spend time here except for occasional strategy meetings. You no doubt favor a warm climate. Say the right word and by this time next week, you will be in a condominium in the Pacific Heights section of Honolulu, looking out one balcony at Diamond Head, the other at Waikiki Beach."

"And I suppose if I play my cards right," Rachel said, "I can have some kind of budget for clothing so that I can look just the way you want me to when you come for a visit."

"The idea crossed my mind. You are attractive, and I am a man."

Carter heard a long sound of disrespect—a Bronx cheer. He suppressed a laugh, stood, replaced his listening device in his wallet, and gathered his weapons. It was time to get out of there.

"You there!" a voice at his rear said. "You don't belong here. Who are you? What are you doing?"

"Bezeidenhout's personal security," Carter said quickly. He turned to look at a large, thick-lipped, bearded man in olive drabs, field boots, and a bright red beret.

"You are one clever son of a bitch to come up with such an answer," the man said, "but it won't wash." He leveled his automatic at Carter. "I am Anders Koven, Bezeidenhout's personal security, and I know nothing at all about you. I think you'd better come along with me." He motioned at Carter with his gun. "You're probably Carter. Wouldn't come in for a little chat, would you? Had to have it entirely your own way, didn't you? Damn! You're the one who blew up the motor pool."

Carter had his weapons and the potential for surprise. Things wouldn't be any better and they could get a lot worse. He started toward Anders Koven, who motioned that Carter toss his weapon down.

Carter tossed his automatic at Koven's knee, caught him a stinging, surprising blow, then launched himself at Koven. He kicked the tender knee and brought a yowl out of the man. From inside the shed, Bezeidenhout heard his security man. "Is that you, Anders? Is everything under control out there?"

The big security man took a swing at Carter with his gun,

clearly wanting to mash him at the kneecap or ankle. Carter did a snap roll to escape a swing from Koven's gun, then leaped at Koven's chest, catching him forcefully with both feet and driving the big man to the ground.

"Answer me, Anders!" Bezeidenhout called.

Anders Koven was about to, but Carter brought out Hugo. Koven's response was a guttural roar of anger.

Carter danced into throwing position and did an underhand toss that caught Koven right where he'd wanted Hugo to go. The throat. The big man tugged at Hugo, got him free with a yank, and saw to his horror that he'd made things as bad for himself as they could get. Blood spurted freely from Koven's throat. The big man could do nothing now but lay there and gurgle.

Piet Bezeidenhout appeared in the doorway, a Luger in his hand. His eyes went from Anders Koven to Carter, catching the situation immediately. "So? Nick Carter, I'd say."

Carter nodded.

"You wouldn't come in. You wouldn't even talk or listen to a proposal. I am a hard man, but in my way I am fair." He spread his hands for a moment as if to demonstrate his fair qualities. "Why would you not even listen? Don't you understand? This is the first organization of its sort. It goes beyond nation and race."

"Does it?" Carter said. "Talk doesn't do much good with people like you. Duvalier in Haiti was so sure of his cause that even when they were overthrowing him, he was trying to explain to them. When a group of peasants staged a protest in Chile, Pinochet was so angered by their point of view that he wanted to have them punished for daring to disagree with the truth—*his* truth."

He could see the prominent vein on Bezeidenhout's forehead begin to throb. "It could have been such a sweet deal for the right people, Carter. It can still develop and have as much power as any organization the world has ever known."

"With you as its head?" Carter asked, shaking his head.

"It was my idea, my plan. Show me someone who is smarter, better prepared for this. I will personally go to that person and make him or her an offer that is the very essence of fairness." His eyes glowed like smoldering coals. "Show me a group like this that has begun with so much money. Most groups have to wait until they are highly successful before they attract financing. I brought large sums from the very beginning."

Carter nodded, a grim frown on his face. "Half that money was ripped off from other sources. It wasn't donated or even lent in good faith. I have very little sympathy for the diamond security forces because I've seen what they've done. But you even stole from them, your own people."

"You don't understand the Afrikaner personality, Carter. They are either very stolid and conservative, or imaginative beyond dreams. Forgetting the problem with the blacks, if you were to take all the money in the country and divide it up equally among the Afrikaners, within a year half of them would be very rich, the other half very poor."

Bezeidenhout watched Anders Koven give a last, convulsive twitch before he died. "Damn you, Carter," he said. "The time is right for Lex Talionis. It's what people want. You see it all over the world. If someone like you came in, if the right people joined, it would be unstoppable."

He thumbed the catch on his Luger, lifted the weapon, and pointed it at Carter. There was no way Carter could get Wilhelmina out or get his hands on his automatic weapon. The only solution was to put as much distance between Bezeidenhout and his Luger as possible. Carter dived for the side of the building and the shadows. Scrambling with his hands and feet, he got more forward motion. The night was split by the roar of Bezeidenhout's Luger firing. The first shot was wide by about ten feet, but the second shot was less than six inches away.

As Carter scrambled to get out of Bezeidenhout's range, the Lex Talionis man squeezed off yet another shot that creased Carter's arm before he got to the darkness and safety.

Bezeidenhout was still firing, calling for help. Carter pulled out Wilhelmina and took off the safety catch. He came around the side of the building in time to meet two LT grunts, each of whom carried an automatic weapon. He shot one before they realized what was happening. The second one tried to take cover, and began cursing when the time came to get the safety off his automatic.

"You've got a choice," Carter called to him. "Leave your weapon and a bandoleer of clips and you're out of here alive."

The LT man seemed to consider this for a moment. "Hey, man, how do I know you ain't jivin' me?"

"I don't want your pistol. Take it and get out of here. You've got five seconds."

The LT man swore, tossed his gun, fumbled in his holster, brought out his .45, and took off into the night. Carter swooped down on the abandoned weapon and checked the safety. Nothing. Carter ejected the clip and saw what the problem was. The first shell in the clip was defective. He pulled it out, snapped the firing pin once, moved the safety, and refitted the clip. He pulled the trigger and had the satisfaction of firing a successful burst.

By the time he got back to the site where he'd left Anders Koven, there was a commotion by a row of vehicles. Unkefer, the man Carter had seen in Belize City, was trying to start Jeeps. One after another failed and Unkefer finally put his hand on his hip and told Bezeidenhout, "Shit, chief, every one of these fuckers has been fixed!"

Bezeidenhout stormed to one of the wide-tread troop transports, got in, and began cranking the ignition. The lumbering vehicle started up and Bezeidenhout began shouting some instructions.

A moment later two men brought out Rachel Porat behind her. She was stuffed into the troop wearing a .45 at each side, have an uphill battle here. This group looked demoralized.

It took Carter twenty minutes to drive the cycle back up to the larger compound. With the exception of the vehicles he and Zachary had disabled, things looked more orderly here, and Carter noticed that guards had been posted outside each building. Before abandoning the cycle and setting out on foot again, Carter looked carefully for sight of the troop transport with Bezeidenhout and Rachel Porat. He saw it in the distance, sitting under the protective light of an arc light, guarded by two men with automatic weapons.

For the moment, everything seemed to be under control with the LT. Carter circled to the east and brought himself behind tree cover that gave him an opportunity to open fire on a small shed. He carefully planned the path he'd take, slipped off the safety on his automatic, and shattered the night with a long burst.

The Lex Talionis people were faster to respond. A group of three men started toward Carter's position. He followed his plan of moving about twenty yards to his right, firing another , then doubling back to his left. He put another long burst he building, then opened up on the building next to it, to give the impression that there were at least two of working on a cross fire. The Lex Talionis men began at Carter's position. Two more LT men told Carter at he wanted to know. The st building in the

Carter heard Bezeidenhout roaring at someone. "I don't care how many of them there are out there, I want you to get them, is that understood?"

The other source of automatic fire was no surprise to Carter. It would have to be the very welcome support of Sam Zachary. On the strength of another burst from the south, Carter zigzagged across the courtyard, risking some fire, but bringing himself within firing range of the main building.

Before he could open up, a spray of automatic fire came from the west. It was not as steady a spray, causing Carter to think the person doing the firing was more of an amateur. Perhaps it was one of Samadhi's teen-agers, he thought.

Carter circled around to see who his latest cohort was. For a moment he was pinned down by two LT soldiers, but help came from the rear. A covering blast drove the LT soldiers off, dropped one of them, and allowed Carter to make his circuit back to the cover of a clump of trees. In a few minutes he was joined by Sam Zachary.

"Who else is out there?"

"I thought you could tell from the irregular but accurate pattern. That's Margo, and I think she has the makings of a natural."

Zachary handed Carter a large metal canister. "One for hands us," he said. "It's from the PLO and it's a fire bomb. I port. Bezeidenhout, now wearing this place up to barbecue level again and the carrier and sped off in an easterly direction.

Carter watched Unkefer for a moment. A group formed men stood around him. "You heard where going," he said to some of them. "You want to compl getting paid and having interesting assignments, place to go."

"Where are you going?" one of them asked.

"I don't know about you guys," Unkefer said, "b bonus to sign on, and I accepted a job. Right now to try to get things cleaned up here and mount som system and run this damned organization like something can be proud of. You guys got any complaints?"

The men stood slack-jawed for a moment, then nodded their heads. "Okay," Unkefer said. "Let's get on with it."

Carter found Koven's corpse, retrieved Hugo, and set out to look for the motorcycle he'd hidden. Unkefer was going to chary who was on his own momentum. Carter began firing and two more LT soldiers made a break into the jungle night. Zachary's fire bomb brought down the front porch and caused a sheet of flame to spread across the building.

They heard a good deal of yelling, and through the smoke Carter saw two men lowering Rachel Porat, trussed and bound, through the window to the ground below. Carter had only a moment to respond, and he was immediately up and running.

Carter reached the heap that was Rachel. He waved the gun at both men who'd lowered her out the window. "Back!" he shouted. "Get back in!" Then he opened up, drawing supportive fire from Margo Huerta.

One of the LT men clutched at his chest, but the other retreated. Carter knew he'd try to get out through another window.

Carter brought out Hugo, slashed the bonds on Rachel, and tossed her Wilhelmina. "That's a good friend. Take care of it."

"Give me a boost," Rachel said, making a gesture of bringing her hands together. Carter understood exactly what she wanted. He made a stirrup of his hands and Rachel bounded from it into the window of the burning building. She was going in after Bezeidenhout.

Carter knew better than that.

He went around toward the back, bumping into an LT soldier who had long since thrown down his guns and now raised his hands at the sight of Carter.

There was a burst of automatic fire, and Bezeidenhout, protected by two men with Kalashnikovs, made a rush toward the secured troop transport. Carter went in pursuit and Bezeidenhout called after him, "You have not seen the end of Lex Talionis so easily, Carter." He showed Carter a large duffel bag. "There are plenty of resources to tide us over, and when the offshore well goes and the airline disaster is seen throughout the world, we will be back as strong as ever." He began laughing maniacally. "I am the law of the lion and I shall have the final say."

He moved closer to the troop transport, his laughter growing even wilder. As he neared the troop transport, there was another sound of laughter, almost like a hyena.

Bezeidenhout stopped, his eyes wide. "Who laughs at me? What is this? Are you laughing, Carter?"

The laugher grew even more scornful, and after a moment it definitely took on the sound of a group of pack animals surrounding their leader.

Bezeidenhout threw the duffel bag into the troop transport and tried to make his departure look dramatic. He slammed the door of the truck and suddenly the laughter changed to a series of gutteral Arabic commands. The guards, all wearing LT uniforms, began to run, trying to put as much distance between themselves and the troop transport as they could.

The driver turned the ignition and the troop transport went up in a loud roar.

For several moments a shower of currency floated downward to the ground, and as it did, Carter and Zachary heard the laughter of Abdul Samadhi.

As the Arab's laughter echoed, all around them the buildings of Lex Talionis burned in the night and the mercenary soldiers faded away one by one.

# TWENTY-ONE

"He got his revenge after all," Carter said.

"Speaking of which," Zachary said, "I'd like to put in for some of my own. You get first choice because you pieced the whole damned puzzle together. But I'd like a shot at Charles Smith. He worked for my people and I'd like the opportunity to scare some revenge out of his eccentric hide."

"Be my guest," Nick Carter said.

Carter drove the Jeep to Dr. Charles Smith's compound. Lights blazed throughout the small building and the eccentric doctor could be heard shouting orders. Zachary went up the stairs first, followed by Carter. Rachel Porat and Margo Huerta waited in the Jeep, their guns ready for any stray die-hard LTs.

Charles Smith, a cold cigar stub clenched between his teeth, looked at them with irritation. "No time for measurements now, fellows. Clearing out of here. This whole deal went unstable."

"It sure did," Zachary said. He pulled out his Luger and began firing at some of Smith's boxes.

"Hey, be careful! They contain valuable medical records and equipment."

Zachary fired a few more shots. Charles Smith stopped, looking at him as though he'd gone mad. "Good," Zachary said, "I've got your attention. Now let's get down to some basics." He took out his wallet and the CIA identity card.

"Oh, hey, no problem," Smith said. "I'm working with you guys."

"Not with me, you aren't, you scumbag. Listen, I know for

186

a fact that you redid a guy from Argentina named Cardenas. God knows how many criminals you've helped with laundered identities."

"Maybe three, four hundred," Smith said. "Nothing personal, just a great medical challenge. I could never see regular cases, not with all those challenges."

"The hell you can't," Zachary said, grabbing him by the collar of his smock. "How much do you make a year? Two, three hundred thou clear?"

"That's peanuts," Smith scoffed.

"Okay," Zachary said. "That's my point. You don't need the money. From now on I want you to go to Third World countries or poverty pockets throughout the world and donate your services for three months a year. If I ever hear of you doing reconstructive surgery for the Company, I will personally track you down and see to it that you need some reconstruction of your own. Do I make myself very clear?" Zachary shot up a few more of Smith's boxes.

"My records!" Smith wailed.

"Do you follow me?" Zachary said.

Smith looked from Zachary to Carter. "You want me not to do any more reconstructs for the CIA. You want me to do charitable works."

"Good charitable works," Zachary emphasized. "People who have been victimized by wars or circumstances beyond their control."

"You CIA people don't all follow the same line, do you."

Zachary smiled. "Some of us are independent thinkers. Some of us get our kicks out of tracking down corrupt cosmetic surgeons and setting them straight."

Dr. Charles Smith looked at the two. "Okay," the diminutive surgeon said. "You've made your point. I'll do charity stuff. Now get out of here and let me pack."

"Gladly," Carter said, leading the way to the Jeep.

An hour later they were back at the Center for the Arts, pounding on Jim Rogan's door.

"What is this?" the poet said. "I thought you guys had left."

"This," Carter said, "is the accounting. I don't know how much you know about Bezeidenhout and his terrorist group, Lex Talionis. We may never know. But we do know that he was helping you with operating capital because you made such a good cover."

"Hey, I had an opportunity and I took it," Rogan said. "I did it for the sake of the arts. It isn't my fault if he got into something unsavory."

Carter shook his head. "Yes, it is your fault and I could nail your ass to the wall on a number of things. You were receiving subsidy payments from Bezeidenhout's sponsors and you were kicking back money to him. That's a laundering device, pure and simple. Well, it's over now. Margo Huerta and Sam Zachary here are going to supervise the finances of this place and if you can't keep your passion for the arts on a more ethical level, we'll take you apart the way we did Bezeidenhout."

"You guys are something else," Rogan said. "You're really going to let us keep the center?"

"Except for one thing," Margo said. "You're the number two man. From now on, you take your orders from me."

"But it was my idea, my dream."

"You sound just like Bezeidenhout," Carter said. "You've got a pretty good deal here. Why don't you go along with it?"

Rogan rubbed his eyes. "This is a lot to take in at once."

Carter stabbed him in the chest with a finger. "Then start taking it in."

Twenty minutes later, after they'd said good-bye to Margo, Carter, Zachary, and Rachel were in the Jeep, headed back to Belize City. "It's not over yet," the Killmaster said. "Bezeidenhout still has those two terror teams out there, intending to do something to the offshore oil rig and some airliner." He looked over at Zachary. "Want in on the assignment?"

"I was thinking I'd take the airline group. I have some pretty good contacts with airline security operations. I can start looking at patterns."

"It's a deal. I'll get the offshore oil group," Carter said. He felt an elbow in his ribs.

"*We'll* get the offshore oil group," Rachel said.

Carter shook his head. "No good. We'd distract each other."

Rachel Porat smiled at him. "You come near me until we've finished this deal and I'll wallop you," she said.

"What about Samadhi and his Beirut street boys?" Zachary said.

Carter was thoughtful. "We'll run into them again some-where. This time, let them go. We owe them one." He en-gaged the gears on the Jeep and roared off toward Belize City.

He had a phone call to make to David Hawk and he had some clean-up work to do on the dirty business that was Lex Talionis.

# DON'T MISS THE NEXT NEW
# NICK CARTER SPY THRILLER

## *HONG KONG HIT*

Delaplane drove around the Cathedral of St. Paul and turned right toward Avenida Almeida Ribiero. Once he hit that main street, he turned left. Two blocks farther on, he swung off the avenue and then turned again into a through alley.

*Paranoid*, he told himself, *you're getting paranoid. You know it now, you've been too long in the life. It's time to quit, to cut and run*. Two days from now, Alice Bradley would have drained the cash from everything. All of it would go into bearer bonds and he would run.

He parked the car in the Osai section and locked it. Far to his right he could see the marquee and lights of the Lisboa Hotel. Carrying the small black bag, he began to walk. The closed shutters and blank windows in the old buildings gave the appearance of desolation. Newspaper and waste cluttered the wet gutters.

But if the outer core was rotting, the inner was solid steel. There were more safes, infrared alarms, and security systems of all kinds to the square inch in Osai than in any other area of Macao. The city's jewelry center. Who would believe it? Only those who had worked there, dazzled by the stones they worked with. It looked like a double string of nineteenth-century poorhouses.

Alone again, the worries that had beset him earlier began to return. Walking up the Avenida Almeida Ribiero, he stopped twice, spending an inordinate length of time peering into Chinese shops, convinced someone was following him. When he sauntered on from the second shop, having become aware that he was studying a heap of powdered boars' tusks, reputedly useful for restoring sexual virility, the belief had become fixed in his mind. Though he recognized no one, he knew someone was following him. Someone close behind, anticipating his curiosity, diving into a doorway or walking away in the opposite direction however quickly he turned. The faces of people who overtook him, the familiar motley array of Chinese, a few Europeans, Americans, and Indians, passed him without a second glance.

He walked on, mopping his face. If only the infernal noise would let up. It thundered ceaselessly into his head, deafening him, a cacophony of trucks and cars, stuttering motorcycles, shrill voices, pedicab bells, the nerve-wracking, never-ending clatter of shoes on the pavements, an exploding scream of darting Chinese children, churning and fusing and booming back from walls along the narrow streets.

Finally he had walked the full circle. He was back, fifty yards from the Lancia. He waited a full five minutes in a doorway. No one paid any attention to him or the car.

He got in and drove directly to the rear of Tai Yang's shop. He parked and doused the lights. He checked the time. Just before midnight.

The rear door was open. He climbed shabby steps to the second floor and checked the street. Quiet. It was gloomy, almost pitch-dark. A night light sprinkled a dappled pattern down the stairs. Delaplane approved. There was just sufficient light to move in safety. He started to climb the stairs, careful not to touch the banister.

He made no effort to tread softly; he was naturally light on his feet. There were three doors on the third landing. The middle one was ajar, subdued light escaping through it. Standing sideways, Delaplane pushed it open with the back of his hand.

A cultured voice called out, "Come in, Mr. Jacobs. You have nothing to fear."

In a strange, contradictory way, Delaplane suddenly felt that he had everything to fear. He stepped into the room.

He wasn't surprised that the light was of low wattage, directed well down. It made a yellow circle on a perfectly clear, leather-topped desk, and the darkness bounced up all around it. Apart from this one oasis of visibility, he couldn't see a thing. The lamp was hypnotic and destroyed his sight in the blacker patches. He could see a shadow behind the desk but no more; not the size of the room, its other furnishings, not even a window.

"Close the door, please."

Delaplane closed the door and Tai Yang moved into the light.

"My workshop is in the rear. Please follow."

Delaplane followed the old man down a narrow corridor into a larger room. There was a large, round workbench in the center of the room. The old man hit a switch and four small but powerful spot lamps lit up the green statue on the black marble base.

"There you are, Mr. Jacobs. The Eye of Ming."

Delaplane set the black case down and walked around and around the statue, inspecting it from every angle. Finally he looked up. "It is exquisite."

"Thank you." Gently the old man tipped the statue up, off its base. "As you requested . . . hollow, lead-lined. The weight, with the marble base, is precisely to your specifications, nineteen ounces shy of the real statue's weight."

"Even with the lead?"

"Yes." Yang set the statue carefully back into the indentation in the base. "This box contains odorless, colorless powdered cement. Simply mix it with water and you can secure the statue to the base forever."

A smile curved Delaplane's lips. "You are truly a craftsman, Mr. Yang."

"Again, thank you. Now, you have brought the remainder of my fee?"

Delaplane set the bag on the workbench and opened it. Using his left hand, he began to stack one-hundred-pound notes beside it. They were clipped ten to a bundle.

As they were set down, Tai Yang picked each one of them up and fanned through them. He was nearly finished, when Delaplane's arm arched into the air. The needle buried itself to the hilt of the hypodermic syringe in the old man's neck, and even before it was completely buried Delaplane was pushing the plunger.

There was some struggle, but very little, as Delaplane

jammed the older body against the bench and held it there until it went limp.

Delaplane, calm now, worked with smooth precision. He stripped everything of value from the body, and then scoured the room for money, gems, anything else of value. Everything he found went into the bag.

This done, he found the crate that Tai Yang had constructed for the statue. It was well padded and indentations had already been molded for the statue and the base. Carefully, he packed both pieces and sealed the crate.

In a corner, he found a two-wheeled handcart. He used this to bring the crate down the two floors and out to the alley door.

The alley was still dark and still deserted. Gently, taking his time, he muscled the crate into the trunk of the Lancia.

Back in the old man's workshop, he pulled on a thin pair of driving gloves and went through the desk. All personal and business papers he threw in the middle of the floor.

From the bag he took a four-ounce strip of plastique and a detonator, and searched for the safe. He found it, embedded in cement, in the floor of the bathroom.

Carefully he packed the hinges and the dial with the plastique, and then inserted the timer-detonator. Then he pulled the mattress, pillow, and blankets off the cot the old man had used to nap on when working late. He packed them tightly over the safe and reached through a narrow opening to turn the spring-wind on the detonator by feel.

The detonator was not a time lock but worked off a single spring. When it was wound, it took exactly sixty seconds to unwind.

Delaplane was in the hallway when the muffled explosion rocked the floor. He waited twenty minutes. When there was no activity from the first floor or the street below, he reentered the room.

He found the acids and several bottles of other highly flammable materials in a refrigerator. These had been used to burn off the impurities in the outer layer of the jade.

Delaplane set them out. By then the smoke had cleared in the bathroom.

In the safe he found five thousand pounds in cash and two trays of precious gems. These went into the bag. All the checkbooks, personal papers, and business records went into the center of the floor. There, they and the body would be the first to burn.

—From HONG KONG HIT
A New Nick Carter Spy Thriller
From Jove in September 1989

## NOBODY DOES IT BETTER THAN

### IAN FLEMING'S

# JAMES BOND

| | |
|---|---|
| ___CASINO ROYALE | 1-55773-256-6/$3.95 |
| ___DIAMONDS ARE FOREVER | 1-55773-215-9/$3.95 |
| ___DOCTOR NO | 1-55773-257-4/$3.95 |
| ___FOR SPECIAL SERVICES* | 1-55773-124-1/$4.50 |
| ___FOR YOUR EYES ONLY | 0-441-24575-7/$3.50 |
| ___FROM RUSSIA WITH LOVE | 1-55773-157-8/$3.50 |
| ___GOLDFINGER | 1-55773-262-0/$3.95 |
| ___ICE BREAKER* | 1-55773-200-0/$4.50 |
| ___LICENSE RENEWED* | 1-55773-201-9/$4.50 |
| ___LIVE AND LET DIE | 0-441-48510-3/$3.50 |
| ___MOONRAKER | 1-55773-185-3/$3.95 |
| ___NOBODY LIVES FOREVER* | 1-55773-210-8/$4.50 |
| ___NO DEALS, MR. BOND* | 1-55773-020-2/$4.50 |
| ___ROLE OF HONOR* | 1-55773-125-X/$4.50 |
| ___THE SPY WHO LOVED ME | 0-441-77870-4/$3.50 |
| ___THUNDERBALL | 1-55773-255-8/$3.95 |

* by John Gardner

---

Check book(s). Fill out coupon. Send to:

**BERKLEY PUBLISHING GROUP**
390 Murray Hill Pkwy., Dept. B
East Rutherford, NJ 07073

NAME_____

ADDRESS_____

CITY_____

STATE_____ZIP_____

**PLEASE ALLOW 6 WEEKS FOR DELIVERY.
PRICES ARE SUBJECT TO CHANGE
WITHOUT NOTICE.**

**POSTAGE AND HANDLING:**
$1.00 for one book, 25¢ for each additional. Do not exceed $3.50.

| | |
|---|---|
| **BOOK TOTAL** | $ ____ |
| **POSTAGE & HANDLING** | $ ____ |
| **APPLICABLE SALES TAX**<br>(CA, NJ, NY, PA) | $ ____ |
| **TOTAL AMOUNT DUE** | $ ____ |

**PAYABLE IN US FUNDS.**
(No cash orders accepted.)

**230**

## HIGH-TECH, HARD-EDGED ACTION!
### All-new series!

___STEELE J.D. Masters 1-55773-219-1/$3.50
Lt. Donovan Steele—one of the best cops around, until he was killed. Now he's been rebuilt--the perfect combination of man and machine, armed with the firepower of a high-tech army! Look for Book Two—*Cold Steele*—coming in November!

___FREEDOM'S RANGERS Keith William Andrews 0-425-11643-3/$3.95
An elite force of commandos fights the battles of the past to save America's future—this time it's 1923 and the Rangers are heading to Berlin to overthrow Adolf Hitler! Look for Book Two—*Raiders of the Revolution*--coming in November!

___TANKWAR Larry Steelbaugh 0-425-11741-3/$3.50
On the battlefields of World War III, Sergeant Max Tag and his crew take on the Soviet army with the most sophisticated high-tech tank ever built. On sale in November.

___SPRINGBLADE Greg Walker 1-55773-266-3/$2.95
Bo Thornton—Vietnam vet, Special Forces, Green Beret. Now retired, he's leading a techno-commando team—men who'll take on the dirtiest fighting jobs and won't leave until justice is done. On sale in October.

___THE MARAUDERS Michael McGann 0-515-10150-8/$2.95
World War III is over, but enemy forces are massing in Europe, plotting the ultimate takeover. And the Marauders—guerrilla freedom fighters—aren't waiting around for the attack. They're going over to face it head-on! On sale in October.

### LOOK FOR THE NEW SERIES—
### COMMAND AND CONTROL—BY JAMES D. MITCHELL
### COMING IN DECEMBER!

---

Check book(s). Fill out coupon. Send to:

**BERKLEY PUBLISHING GROUP**
390 Murray Hill Pkwy., Dept. B
East Rutherford, NJ 07073

NAME_____

ADDRESS_____

CITY_____

STATE_____ZIP_____

**PLEASE ALLOW 6 WEEKS FOR DELIVERY.
PRICES ARE SUBJECT TO CHANGE
WITHOUT NOTICE.**

**POSTAGE AND HANDLING:**
$1.00 for one book, 25¢ for each additional. Do not exceed $3.50.

| | |
|---|---|
| **BOOK TOTAL** | $_____ |
| **POSTAGE & HANDLING** | $_____ |
| **APPLICABLE SALES TAX** (CA, NJ, NY, PA) | $_____ |
| **TOTAL AMOUNT DUE** | $_____ |

**PAYABLE IN US FUNDS.**
(No cash orders accepted.)